ECHOES OF BETRAYAL

PROTOCOL CLEAN SLATE

J. Henry Tate

Publishers Note:
This is a work of fiction. All names, characters, places, and
events are the work of the author's imagination. Any
resemblance to real persons, places, or events is coincidental.

J. Henry Tate ©2024

Solstice Publishing

www.solsticepublishing.com

ACKNOWLEDGMENT

I must first acknowledge God as the giver of the gift that allowed me to complete "Echoes of Betrayal: Protocol Clean Slate." The first person to recognize the gift God had given me was an English Comp instructor who asked me to write for 'Vox Populi' the college newspaper.

After college, William Smothers of Spikin Out News, and Cathey Carney of the Old Huntsville Magazine, both provided an outlet for my budding talent.

In writing this book, I would not have completed it without the support of my sweet wife Bertha. Who reminded me I was working on it when we got married twenty-four years ago. Thank you sweetness for your support and encouragement.

Thank you to Vicki Al-Hakeem for your editing and proofreading early on. Thank you to my beta readers John Burris, WK Smith, Judy and Stew Stewart, MD Smith, Tommy and Barbara Beal, Barbara Kirk, Felicia Kirk, Adam Martin, Helen Harrand, and Martha Bradas.

Each of you brought a unique viewpoint and perspective to the novel. Thank you for doing your part to get the best out of me. Last, but certainly not least, I say thank you to Melisa Miller, of Solstice Publishing, for your belief in this book.

DEDICATION

"Echoes of Betrayal: Protocol Clean Slate" was inspired by true events. Dennis Depew is the boss's name in real life. Daniel, the name used in the novel is the name of Dennis' youngest son.

Dennis died on the operating table three times the night he was shot, but they were able to bring him back. When they finally sent him home, he had a mesh inside of his stomach to keep his insides in. His odds of living six months were not good. That was nearly thirty years ago.

Over the years, he had to be rushed to the hospital several times a year to save his life. Did I mention they said he was never to walk again?

Not only did the ex-Navy Seal walk, he also went fishing with his kids, bought a condo in Florida with his wife Mitzi, and saw three of his grandchildren be born. I started writing the true story in 1994. The nonfiction story needed approval, and verification, from the State Department, Department of Defense, and even the State of Alabama.

In 2019, I decided to turn the manuscript into a novel, inspired by true events. That was when things began to move. Dennis died in 2021, but not before I got to share the first unedited draft of Protocol Clean Slate with him. He passed away at home with his family around him. I sanitized down, put on my mask because of COVID-19, and was able to see him a couple of days before his death.

I am with a publisher who helped me to produce a book worthy of my friend's trust in me as a writer. Dennis will not see the final book, however, Mitzi, his widow, and the other family members will know he was my inspiration.

CHAPTER ONE

MILE MARKER 113

Relieved to be in his private sanctuary, and looking forward to a long quiet weekend, private investigator Jack Campbell kicked his front door closed behind him. He lugged the case of Budweiser beer and bags of snacks through his living room to the kitchen. The cold air conditioning, although a welcome relief from the famously humid Alabama air, gave him a little shiver.

Jack had taken on extra cases during his boss Daniel Draper's month-long absence. Daniel had been working on an insurance case in Texas. He was due back later that night, but Jack's only concern was a relaxing evening with cold beer, snacks, and HBO movies.

Pulling a cold sweaty can of Budweiser from the fridge, he could smell the Budweiser as the hiss of pressure escaped the popped tab. *No need to wait*, he thought, taking a sip while putting away the snacks.

This Friday night wasn't like those of nearly a year ago when he managed a restaurant. The mere thought triggered a tension headache, a lingering effect from past migraines.

"Not tonight," He said to himself. "Cold Budweiser, a good movie, and no stress."

Jack couldn't lay his finger on the excitement he was feeling until he thought about the times back in high school. He had not felt this type of excitement since he and his best friend, Daniel Draper, would go out partying on Friday and Saturday nights.

He considered himself lucky to work with Daniel, who unexpectedly reappeared almost a year ago, nearly fifteen years after leaving town.

Over the last seven or eight months, Jack found joy in his new career. Warm feelings enveloped him as he thought about the dinner with the Draper family the next night. Dinner with Daniel, his wife Becky, and their two boys promised laughter and fun.

Jack imagined the round table in the Draper's kitchen, with all of the food, and a big glass of Becky's sweet iced tea in hand. Smiling, he thought about how sweet Becky made her tea, so sweet he could feel the cavities growing in his mouth.

Saturday night would be entertaining. For a moment, he thought about Becky's shiny red hair, the way it seemed to shimmer as she went back and forth to the kitchen. As he did regularly, he pushed the image out of his mind. After all, no good could come of dwelling on her beauty.

But that was tomorrow; tonight's agenda was to melt into his stuffed sofa with cold Budweiser until he fell asleep. Wiping his hand on his pant leg, he flopped down on the sofa. "Seven o'clock, what's coming on next?" he said aloud as if someone else was in the room.

After a long swig of beer, shaking the can, he headed to the fridge for another. The ringing phone startled him. Looking at his watch, he walked over to the kitchen counter and picked up the cordless phone. An unexplained chill ran down his back, as Becky Draper's panicked voice stopped him in his tracks.

"Becky, Becky, please slow down, what's wrong?!"

Panic was starting to bubble up in Jack, trying to maintain his composure, once again he asked, "What's wrong?

"Somebody shot Daniel!" Taking another breath, "Did you hear me? Somebody shot Daniel!"

The words didn't make sense, it was all of a sudden a surreal moment for Jack. He had never had an out-of-body experience, but at that very moment, he was feeling separated from himself, his head spun, and he was dazed by the words that he could not connect.

Hearing Becky in such distress shook him, and his breathing became erratic as he tried to catch his breath. The buzz from the beer was all but gone, however, the two beers still slowed his ability to get his thoughts together.

The lump in his throat was as if someone had shoved their fist down his throat, and dared him to breathe. His mind was racing trying to find a handle on the reality that seemed to be just beyond his reach.

"Jack! We're at the hospital, I need you now!" Becky yelled, with a very noticeable tremble in her voice.

These words forced him to focus. "I'm on my way!" Were the only words he could muster as he hung up the phone. The phone made a rattling sound as he put it down because his hands were shaking, but he had no time to think about it now.

He had never known anybody who had been shot before, what do he do now? Ok, Becky is waiting for him at the hospital, and she needs him. Suppose Daniel dies, can he give Becky and the boys the support they need?

Jack, snap out of it, I must be the tower of strength Becky needs. He thought as he grabbed his keys from the kitchen counter. As he rushed past the end table, next to the sofa, as he headed to the front door, Jack knocked everything on the table to the floor.

This was a regular occurrence, just out of instinct, he hurriedly picked up everything, except a pen that rolled a foot away from the table. He placed the items back on the table and he was out the door.

Everything seemed to be a blur, Jack did not remember getting on the interstate, and it was not until he glanced down to check his gas that he realized that he was driving 95 miles per hour. At that speed, the hospital was still over twenty minutes away, which at the time seemed like a lifetime.

As the fog in Jack's mind started clearing, he began to mentally ask himself some questions.

Who shot Daniel?

Was he back home when he was shot?

Was it because of the case in Texas?

As he was starting to focus on the questions, settling in for the twenty-minute drive, but most of all preparing himself for what he would find at the hospital, his cell phone rang. He had forgotten that the cell phone was in his shirt pocket.

The sudden sound caused him to jump, and swerve his car to the right a little bit. He answered with some irritation in his voice.

"Hello!"

"Is this Jack Campbell?" Asked the official-sounding female voice on the other end.

With hesitation in his voice he replied, "Yes, it is,"

"Mr. Campbell, a State Trooper, is standing by at mile marker 113 headed North, he will lead you to the hospital."

"I don't understand. What trooper? Why… what is going on?!"

"Mr. Campbell, all will be explained to you at the hospital."

With that, the phone went dead. Any remaining buzz Jack had was completely gone now. While trying to wrap his head around the phone call, at that moment it occurred to him, *Where are all the cars?*

He could not see any car lights in any direction, *That's odd,* he thought, *It's just after 7:15 p.m., no later than 7:30.*

Blue lights were flashing off in the distance. Getting closer, he could see a State Trooper's car parked on the side of the road. Closer still, he could see that the Trooper was parked at mile marker 113.

Jack slowed down to pull up to him, but the State Trooper took off, wheels spinning – throwing gravel and waving his arm out of the window for Jack to follow.

Jack had to push to stay with him, looking down at the speedometer, they were driving 110 miles per hour. To Jack, this was both a little exciting, and scary at the same time.

There was a surreal feeling of driving so fast, and yet at the same time, things seemed to be moving so slowly. Keeping up with the State Trooper was somewhat of a challenge, not because of the speed, but because he could not stay focused.

He could not help thinking about the pain Daniel must have been in. *I wonder will he still say it only hurts for a little while?*

Driving by the next exit, he now understood why there were no cars on the interstate. State Troopers and County Sheriff's Deputies had the interstate on-ramps blocked to traffic. Jack and his State Trooper had the interstate to themselves.

What the hell? Now Jack was worried.

Was Daniel already dead?

What else was going on?

Why are we getting all this attention?

Entering downtown Huntsville, the city cops had also blocked the intersections, allowing Jack and the State Trooper to pass through without stopping.

What the hell, even the intersections inside the city have been blocked off. This can't be good, Daniel must be in really bad shape if they need me to get there so fast.

He saw the Trooper's car put on the left turning flasher, and just that quickly they were already at the hospital parking lot. Jack followed the State Trooper to the emergency entrance, where they parked next to the ambulances.

Jack started to get out of his car but was surprised when a city police officer pushed his car door close.

"Please stay in the car sir." The officer said.

"What is going on, why do I need to stay in my car?"

"Someone will be with you in a moment, and all will be explained."

It was only a couple of minutes, but it seemed like a lifetime sitting in his car, with no one talking to him. Two men, dressed in dark suits, who later turned out to be Feds, came over to him and opened his car door.

One of the men said, "Sir, when you get out of the car, please walk between the two of us into the building."

He tried asking them questions, "Sir, all will be explained to you by someone inside. But for now, we must move quickly." It was all he could do to keep up.

Entering through the emergency room entrance, Jack could see the waiting room almost to capacity, with some waiting patients seemingly resigned to the fact that they would be there most of the night. Others seemed to have hope reflected on their faces.

Jack always hated the smells, sights, and sounds in a hospital. Along with the smell of disinfectant, the lights were so bright a blind man could see, and it seemed that the air-conditioning was always turned down to thirty degrees. As the automatic doors to the emergency waiting room opened and closed, the sounds of ambulances coming were clear.

Although the ambulances would cut the sirens off at the entrance to the parking lot, they could still be heard for several blocks as they approached the hospital.

Entering the waiting elevator, the man on Jack's right pushed a button. When the elevator stopped, the number above the door showed they were on the 3rd floor, and the sign on the opposing wall showed the location to be the surgery waiting room. The man on the right motioned for Jack to step out.

As they stepped into the waiting room, everyone looked to see who was getting out of the elevator. There were police officers there, and they all took slightly defensive postures as they evaluated Jack and the two men coming off of the elevator.

With disbelief and amazement on his face, Jack scanned the waiting room. The police had divided the waiting room into two sections, with several city cops forming a line separating the two sections.

Stepping in, Jack could see that Daniel's family was in one section of the waiting room by themselves. Once again, the nagging question came back.

What the hell is going on?

Walking slowly toward Daniel's family, Jack could see Becky and their sons Matthew, nine years old, and Noah, seven years old, Becky's parents and Daniel's mom.

There were other family members in a smaller cluster to one side, but Jack did not see Daniel's two brothers and sister, his sister Gina was the oldest, Bobby was older than Daniel, and Billy was the baby of the family.

Some family members were sobbing softly, and others were just sitting or standing with sad and defeated looks on their faces. Jack still could not tell if Daniel was alive or dead.

Seeing Jack walking toward the family, Becky ran to meet him. Her red hair against her fair skin shimmered as she ran. He felt ashamed of himself for thinking of her hair at a time like this.

Even at a distance, he could tell she had been crying a lot, and upon seeing him, the faucet opened again.

"Jack!"

Calling his name, she wrapped her arms around his neck, burying her face into his shoulder, and just cried. It was a little hard for him to breathe because her grip was so tight around his neck.

He just held her, without saying a word, until she turned him loose. Keeping her safe was the only thing on his mind now.

"Jack, somebody shot my Daniel, and no one will tell me anything. My family is under police protection, and they're going to have an unmarked car outside our home.

Becky was speaking in rapid fire, Jack tried to catch what she was saying and waited for her to take a breath. Finally, she was quiet, except for the sniffing sound from crying.

Before Jack could ask her questions, a tall bureaucrat-looking man came up to them. Jack surmised that he was a Fed based on his appearance.

"Hi, my name is Robert Reed, and I'm with the State Department."

"The State Department?!" Jack asked while looking at Becky as if expecting her to answer.

"Please come with me, your questions will be answered."

The two of them followed Reed to a room just down the hall. The walk away from the general waiting area was a short one but emotionally it was a world away. The somber tone of the general waiting area was replaced with a more muted tone of anxiety.

They were taken to a room; the door was open with two plainclothes men standing on either side of the door.

Jack's curiosity started to outrank his fear. His investigative mind started to take notes, and the checklist in his head grew as they approached the room.

Daniel was shot,

Some woman called my cell phone,

A State Trooper escorted me to the hospital,

The interstate was closed to all other traffic,

City intersections were blocked off by city cops,

A whole section of the surgery waiting room was blocked off for Daniel's family,

Plainclothes, Federal Guards.

Before completing his mental list, they entered the door, which was a private waiting area, with much more comfortable chairs and sofas. In the middle of the room, was a slender well-dressed woman in a gray-skirt business suit and there was a man dressed in an expensive-looking blue suit.

Approaching with her hand extended to Becky, the woman introduced herself.

"Hi Mrs. Draper and Mr. Campbell, I'm Mary Rogers." Simultaneously, she nodded at Mr. Reed, and he left the room.

Becky took the extended hand and felt its coldness. She didn't know why that stood out to her at a moment like that. She had stopped crying, but her perception of her surroundings was still foggy.

Jack recognized the woman's voice. "It was you on the phone?"

"Yes, Mr. Campbell, I was the one who called you to let you know about the State Trooper escort." She continued, "I'm your liaison with the State Department."

Rogers was well put together, with strong European features, she looked like a how-to-poster for government women's dress codes. Nodding toward the man in the blue suit, "This is Dr. Fredericks, the Hospital Director of Public Relations.

My job is to help you through this process as we try and find out who shot Mr. Draper, and Dr. Fredericks will keep us apprised of Daniel's medical condition."

Something about Dr. Fredericks didn't fit, but Jack couldn't figure it out. Dr. Fredericks' name badge had "Director of Public Relations" under his name. He assumed the Dr. attached to his name was Ph.D. since there were no other professional notations on Fredericks's badge.

Dr. Fredericks wore a very expensive suit, and yet he didn't seem to fit. Fredericks being present brought up even more questions in Jack's mind. Becky and Jack just looked at each other. The checklist of strange things in Jack's mind just got larger.

The State Department,

Director of Public Relations for the hospital,

All because of a small-town private eye being shot.

"I need to sit down," Becky said quietly, reaching for Jack's arm. Ms. Rogers directed them to a black leather sofa and offered to get them something to drink. To Rogers' surprise, Becky snapped at her

"No, I don't want nothing to drink, just tell me what in the hell is going on! My husband has been shot, and we don't know who did it! Even more confusing, why in the hell is the federal government here?"

With a softness in her voice and as much compassion as she could muster, Rogers asked Dr. Fredericks to update them on Daniel's status as of that point and give any prognosis that he could provide. Rogers and Dr. Fredericks sat in two chairs in front of Jack and Becky.

"Well," he started, "Mr. Draper received a gunshot wound to the lower abdomen, just to the right side. The bullet had an explosive element to it and this has created some serious challenges for the surgeons. At this time, I can only say that he is in surgery, and we are doing everything to save his life. The Chief of Surgery and the Lead Trauma Doctor are working on him together."

"I cannot provide any additional information at this time. However, I'll update you when I have something new to tell you." Looking at Mary Rogers, "Ms. Rogers asked me to keep you informed, as news becomes available."

"Thank you, Doctor," Rogers said, as she stood and shook his hand, dismissing him before any questions could be asked, "We will expect to hear updates as soon as you get them. Make sure you speak to no one before you speak to me first. Do you understand?" He said he did and promptly left the room.

He did not show any outward signs, but Dr. Fredericks was upset by the way Rogers dismissed him. Earlier that afternoon, Dr. Fredericks was looking forward to a planned weekend off with his wife.

As the Director of Public Relations for a regional hospital, his days were full of putting out potential public relations fires and trying to protect the hospital from lawsuits. He had cleared his desk and checked to see if any emails could not wait until Monday.

As he logged off his computer, his office phone rang. He started to let it go to voicemail, it was well after the time he was supposed to have left. But he was a man of duty, so he picked up the phone, and with a notable sigh, he said, "This is Dr. Fredericks, how may I assist you?"

"Dr. Fredericks, this is Mary Rogers."

Clearing his throat, "Yes ma'am, how may I assist you?"

Rogers continued, "There is a highly valued patient being transported to your hospital, his name is Daniel Draper. He will require the GSW trauma team with the Head of Surgery operating. Mr. Draper is to have whatever medical resources available, with no consideration given to cost."

"We manage gunshot wounds every day," Fredericks said, "there is no need to get the head of surgery for that."

With some firmness in her voice, Rogers said, "This is a national security issue, and the State Department has determined that the head of surgery and the head trauma doctors will work on Mr. Draper. Once he is out of surgery, you will move Mr. Draper to the private suite. Are we clear?"

"I understand, I'll take care of everything."

After hanging up the phone, Dr. Fredericks started making calls. The first was to the attending doctor in the emergency room, giving instructions on whom to call in. Fredericks also told him that he would call the Head of Surgery himself.

Dr. Fredericks called Dennis McGee, the Head of Security, and informed him that a high-priority GSW was coming in. Fredericks asked McGee to get city police officers to cordon off a section of the surgery waiting room for the patient's family.

Next, Dr. Fredericks called Sally, his wife. "Hi hon, an important emergency patient is coming in, and I must stay at the hospital. I might have to stay the whole weekend."

Sally gave a long sigh, "Honey, it's been months since we had a weekend together, and you deserve the time off. Can't someone else cover for you?"

Fredericks took a deep breath and said, "Mary Rogers called."

"Oh, I understand, I love you, and please be careful."

"I love you too. We will take some time off as soon as we can."

Sally understood that when Mary Rogers called, her husband had to drop everything. A little over five years ago, Dr. Fredericks was a doctor in the Navy and had gotten himself in trouble by taking some drugs from the VA hospital without permission.

He was heading for some jail time and a dishonorable discharge from the Navy. At the last moment, Mary Rogers stepped in, kept him out of jail, and got him honorably discharged from the Navy with his pension intact.

He had no idea who she was and why she helped him. However, she got all charges dropped, and he had to leave the Navy right away; he got to retire with full benefits and have no marks on his records. He could work in the associated healthcare field but not as a doctor or have anything to do with patient care or prescription medication.

Rogers even arranged his position with the Regional Hospital in Huntsville, Alabama. As the Director of Public Affairs, he only reported to the Board of Directors. Fredericks was the second-highest authority in the hospital, second only to the Director of Operations, and above the highest-ranking medical doctors.

Fredericks never did find out why Mary Rogers intervened on his behalf, her only condition was that when she called, he would do whatever she asked. It was not until a year after he had left the Navy that he learned that she was with the State Department. She had called a couple of times to ask him to get some information on a patient in the hospital, but he never asked why, nor did she offer any explanations.

Today was the first time Rogers called with such a dramatic and high-priority request. But as promised, he did what she asked. With these things going through his mind as he was leaving the room, he thought, *How could this woman dismiss me as if I were an orderly?*

After Dr. Fredericks left the room, Rogers said, "Excuse me." Walking to the door, someone handed her two cans of Sprite, and she brought them over, giving the unopened cans to Jack and Becky.

"Let's see if we can figure this all out. Becky, is it OK if I call you Becky?"

"That's OK. Do you know who shot my husband?" Becky asked as she fought to hold herself together.

Rogers reached out and touched Becky's arm, "No, we don't, but with your and Jack's help, maybe we can figure it out."

"How can we help?" Jack asked sharply, "We don't know a damn thing, and have no idea why the State Department is involved. Lady, someone needs to tell us what is going on!"

Mary Rogers sighed and sat back in her chair, she looked at Becky and Jack, moving her head back and forth very slowly.

"Close the door, please!" she yelled at the two men outside the room. One of them reached inside and closed the door.

Mary slid closer to Jack and Becky, and said, "What I'm about to tell you, is classified and must remain in this room with us. Do you understand?" They both nodded their heads, with their full attention focused on Mary Rogers.

Taking a deep breath, leaning in, she said, "My office reached out to Daniel several days ago regarding some information that came to our attention, the information is regarding our nation's security. He was to provide some additional information once he got home this weekend.

He was in the middle of leaving a message for me when he was shot."

"What information?" Becky asked, "So he was on the phone with you when he got shot?"

"No, not me, my assistant, Daniel was leaving a message for me."

"About what?" Jack asked, with his head tilted to one side, like of puppy seeing something unfamiliar.

"We don't know," Mary continued, "This is what we know, he called in at about 5:30 pm, your local time. His message said that he would get the information I requested out of storage and have it overnighted to my office on Monday. There was a loud bang as he talked, and his cell phone was cut off."

"We learned that someone shot Daniel in your home's driveway by monitoring the local emergency channels. I was on the State Department Jet, and I had the pilot change direction and head this way. While in the air, I coordinated with the FBI, your Governor's office, who made all state law enforcement resources available to us."

Something did not add up for Jack, there had to be more than what the Rogers woman told them. *Why would she have the jet change directions, after such a brief message?* For now, he just stored that question away, along with the others.

Rogers asked Becky to recount what had happened in the last few hours. Becky took a moment to steady herself. Drawing in a deep breath and letting it out.

"Okay," She started, "The boys and I had been in very good moods all day because we were looking forward to this night.

"Daniel would be home after being away for nearly a month, working a case. Since Daniel opened his own Private Investigation company, he has been on the road a lot."

"Noah and Matthew were running around making all kinds of noise, but I gave them a little leeway because I knew they were excited about Dad coming home. I looked out of the dining room window and saw Daniel pull my car into the driveway."

With a surprised look on her face, Mary interrupted her, "Your car? Don't you mean his car?"

"No, his car is in the shop, he had to use mine for this trip. We were going to pick his car up from the shop tomorrow morning."

Mary said, "Okay," as she asked Becky to continue.

Both Jack and Becky noted that for the first time, Mary Rogers took a little notepad out of her pocket and started to make notes. Jack made a mental note about her note-taking. *There must be something about what Becky said.*

Continuing with her recount of the afternoon, Becky said, "I told the boys to wash up, their dad was in the driveway, and I want us ready to eat once he got in."

"Did you notice anything out of the ordinary?" Mary interrupted.

Becky shook her head slowly, with a questioning look on her face, "I saw Daniel pull up to his regular parking spot as I turned back to the stove to check the pots. I started putting ice into the glasses and glanced up to see Daniel sitting in the car talking on his cell phone."

"After filling the glasses with tea and putting the pitcher back in the fridge, I said out loud, 'OK, enough is enough, he needs to get in here before the dinner gets cold.'"

"I turned to call Matthew to go out and get Dad, I heard a bang, much louder than a powerful M-80 firecracker. I turned and looked out the dining room window, and Daniel was out of the car, sitting on the ground, with his back up against the car."

"I said, 'What the hell,' under my breath. By now, both boys were looking out the dining room window with me. Daniel's head turned slowly toward the house, his eyes looked directly into mine, and I knew. I don't know how I knew it, but I yelled for Matthew to call 911 and tell them that someone shot his dad. I ran out of the kitchen door towards him and ..."

Becky broke down in tears, as Jack wrapped his arms around her, feeling her trembling in his arms. Mary gave Becky a moment to compose herself, and then she asked, "Did anything strange happen while Daniel was away?"

At first, Becky said no, but for some reason, her credit card and car rental came to mind.

"I don't know whether it was strange or not, but I called Enterprise Car Rental to rent a minivan because Daniel's car was in the shop, and Matthew, our eldest son, had a field trip. I had committed to driving and chaperoning several of his classmates. The only credit card at the house was the one with my maiden name on it."

"Enterprise said the card must have my married name on it. So, I called the card company and updated my information. The actual call only lasted fifteen minutes. They asked me for the answers to the security questions I sat up years ago. They updated my security questions to include the make and model of my car."

"Once the update was completed, I asked that the card be Fed-Exed to me overnight, they agreed and said the charge would be added to the new card. The strange thing, within an hour of that call, I got a call from a man who said he was in the security department for the card company."

"He explained that since it had been years since I used the card, and since my name had been changed, he wanted to make sure I was the right person. The call only lasted five minutes, but the questions were more about my time in the Air Force and when I left the service. That is the closest thing to strange I can think of."

Mary Rogers sat quietly for a moment, looking at her notes, and then she looked up at Jack and Becky. Without saying a word, she stood up and walked to the door. After she whispered something to one of the men standing guard, they both looked back at Becky and Jack and then left the room.

CHAPTER TWO
DISAPPEARING INK

Becky, Jack, and Mary Rogers spent five hours in the private waiting room, which resembled an upscale office space. The wall colors were a muted mauve, with some sort of pale green border.

Initially oblivious, Jack later caught the soft strains of calming music from hidden speakers. Glancing at Becky, he noticed the soothing impact on her. He silently acknowledged, *The music thing works.*

Becky had a different sense of the private waiting room. In the Air Force, she traveled all around the world and became very familiar with upscale art, and craft furniture. The art and furniture, evident replicas, lacked quality.

She heard the music long before Jack did. Her early awareness of the music, likely a result of Air Force security training, showcased her heightened environmental awareness. Funny, she hadn't thought about her security training for nearly fifteen years, but the events of the day brought back memories she had long buried.

For the most part, Becky could tell that the soft-beneath surface music was having a calming effect on Jack. He was able to control the rage he held below the surface. But that feeling didn't last long.

Rogers asked one more question before answering a question Jack had asked. The calming music had met its match. The emotional temperature reached a new high. Turning to Mary Rogers, with a stare Becky had never seen before (but Daniel had told her about) Jack spoke.

"We have been in this damn room for a long while. Do you think Becky and I know something we are not telling you?"

As if her job was to poke the bear, Rogers asked, "Did Daniel ever speak to either of you about his work in the Navy?"

"That's it!" Jack yelled, "We are done with you and your bullshit! You may go and do whatever job you are supposed to be doing to find out who shot Daniel."

Leaning in a little, Mary said quietly, "I know this is tough on the both of you. Jack, I have two jobs at the moment. The first is to make sure that you and Daniel's family are safe. The second is to find out who did this and why."

With that, she asked, "Did Daniel ever have any strange visitors right after he was discharged from the Navy?" Looking at Jack, with a little exacerbation in her voice, Becky said, "None that I recall."

For the first time, the last question asked by Rogers raised Becky's heartbeat a little. Daniel had been very open with Becky, about some of his missions as a Navy Seal. But there was one mission that concerned Daniel. He never gave any details, but he was concerned that he may be on someone's wet-works list. (Wet work was killing.)

What, and when was that mission? Could this shooting be because of that mission? What did... Rogers asked another question, bringing Becky out of her deep thought.

"How about in the last few days," Mary said, with a puzzling look at Becky. "Any strange people hanging around the house?"

Jack threw his hands up. "Damn it, that's it!"

Looking into Jack's eyes, Becky called his name in a quiet voice. "Jack." The impact of her voice was immediate. No matter what was going on, Becky seemed to always get Jack to calm down, even when Daniel couldn't.

Jack continued with a calmer tone, "Every time we ask you a question, you ask three more questions instead of answering. Finally, will you tell us what is going on?"

Just then, the door opened, and Dr. Fredericks stepped inside. He motioned for Mary to come over to him. Becky and Jack strained to try and hear what was being said.

Becky grabbed Jack's arm and held it so tight, that Jack could feel her blood pumping through her hand. He placed his other hand on top of Becky's hand, to provide comfort and strength all at the same time.

After what seemed like a long time to Jack and Becky, but was only a couple of moments, Mary turned with a slight smile on her face as she and Dr. Fredericks walked over to them.

With a smile on her face, Mary said, "Go ahead doctor, tell them the good news."

"I spoke to the surgery team," Dr. Fredericks started while smiling at Becky, "The surgeons said that they are 90% through with the surgery and that Daniel is now stable."

Dr. Fredericks continued, "They expect him to be in surgery for another hour or two. At that time, Daniel will be moved to Intensive-Care recovery."

Becky could hardly control her excitement, still holding on to Jack's arm, she bounced like a little girl as she heaved a sigh of relief, "When can I see my husband?"

Dr. Fredericks replied, "You will be able to see him after he is out of recovery. They have his private room ready, and you are welcome to wait in the room for him."

Mary spun quickly and said, "I'll talk to you in the room later, I must go and set up security protocols for when Daniel is moved to his room." With that, she gave Dr. Fredericks' arm a little tug, and they left Becky and Jack standing in the middle of the room, still a little confused, and with more questions than answers.

"OK, that was good news, right?" Jack said in a soft, tentative whisper.

"Well, the doctor did say he was stable and should be out of surgery in one to two hours," Becky said, as she smiled at the glimmer of hope.

Jack, felt himself simmering under the surface.

"But Mary left out of here so fast, and we still don't know any more than we did five hours ago."

When Jack walked to the door, one of the two men still outside the door, turned to him and said, "Sorry Sir, you and Mrs. Draper must stay in the room until Ms. Rogers gives us further instructions."

"Do you know what is going on?" Jack said trying to get information from the man talking, "And why is there all this security for a small-time private eye?"

Looking directly at Jack, "Sir, you must stay in the room until we receive further instructions from Ms. Rogers."

Although his words were kind and friendly, his look was anything but. Jack decided it was best not to push this guy, so he turned and went back to Becky.

She looked at Jack, and with the strength she was known for starting to come through, she said, "You have worked closely with my husband for nearly a year, and he has trained you well. He taught you everything you know about ferreting out information and gathering resources.

It's time for you to take the lead." Looking directly into Jack's eyes, as if they were sharing each other's strength, she continued, "He said you're the best he's seen, your natural ability to spot bullshit and uncover secrets is second to none. Now I want you to do what you do."

Nodding toward the door, she continued. "Find out what this damn woman is not telling us and find out who shot my husband. Are you ready for this?"

After he nodded his head, she put her finger under Jack's chin, and said with a strong, quiet voice, "I'm counting on you to get through this."

With no other words, and with all of the commitment needed, Jack simply said, "I got you."

Becky continued, "You and I know what Daniel did in the Navy, and we know that they can't know that we know, it's best for all of us. We must also assume they are tapping all our phones and monitoring our internet."

"I want you to treat this as a case, with me as your handler, I'll curate information as you gather it, and then we will use our tools to find the truth."

Jack nodding in agreement, said, "I'll get a couple of those new prepaid phones and use our safety deposit box at the Independent Security Box Service. That way, the data we gather is safe."

"Good idea Jack, also set up a couple of new AOL email accounts. There is no way you will get out of here now, we must wait until we are in the private room. We must keep each other updated if we have any conversations with anybody."

In a soft voice, Jack asked, "Do you remember the invisible ink pens Daniel got us as a joke? Do you still have yours?"

Becky nodded and said, "I carry several in my purse to keep the kids entertained."

"Good, when we are in the room and need to communicate something, we will use the pens."

After Rogers left the private waiting room, she met with Robert Reed. "Reed, do we know any more about the shooting than we did five hours ago?"

"No," Reed responded, "The locals have nothing, the FBI has no leads, and our office said there have not been any new developments regarding John Lasher."

"I feel sorry for these people," Rogers showing any emotions for the first time, "I like Becky, if we had met some other way, she would be like my little sister. Jack, on the other hand, takes a little getting used to.

But I can tell, he is loyal, and Becky trusts him. OK, our job is to keep them alive and find out who is behind this."

After talking to Reed, Rogers entered a room and closed the door. After thirty minutes, Mary Rogers left the audio surveillance room, she wrote in her notepad, *Independent Security Box Service,* and pens.

When she returned to the private waiting room, she had Matthew and Noah with her. She explained, "I have briefed the family members waiting in the waiting room and asked that they go home. I promised each would be contacted with updates as information became available."

Becky asked, "How will you be able to update everyone?"

"We got the names and contact information for everyone in the waiting room, that way, we can contact them directly with updates."

Jack and Becky looked at each other, knowing the real reason for getting everyone's name and contact information. Mary escorted Becky, the two boys, and Jack to the private room that had been prepared for Daniel.

Bodyguards had already been stationed at different points in the hallway near Daniel's room, near the elevators and exit stairs. This room was unlike any other private hospital room they had ever seen.

It was a little suite like you might find in a Days Inn Hotel, and the hospital bed area had an attached bathroom, and a TV mounted on the wall at the foot of the bed, like any other hospital room.

However, the sitting area was like an upscale waiting room with a sofa, a dining room table for six, and two recliners, the sofa also had a fold-away bed, and there was a separate bathroom for guests.

The entertainment area had board games and some video games for kids. The little kitchenette area included a small refrigerator, two-eyed stovetop, and microwave. Becky checked the fridge and cabinets and was amazed by how full they were.

It was then that Becky realized that they had not eaten dinner, and now that the adrenaline was dropping, they were all very hungry. She didn't feel like cooking anything, so she opened the door, and asked one of the men, "Who do we contact to get something to eat? No one has eaten dinner, and it is after 1:00 a.m."

"There's a kitchen dedicated to these hospital suites," The man said, "and is operational 24/7. All you have to do is pick up the phone and dial the number 7."

After providing the information to Becky, the man closed the door. Becky picked up the phone, but before she could dial 7, someone picked up. "Yes, Mrs. Draper, my name is Alice, how may I assist you?" Said the friendly female voice on the other end.

"Hi Alice, We have been in the hospital for six or seven hours, and we haven't eaten dinner. What kind of things can you fix at this time?"

"Mrs. Draper, we are a fully functioning kitchen and can prepare, cook, and bake almost anything you would like. We can fix breakfast, lunch, dinner, or a combination of all menus if needed."

After thinking for a moment Becky said, "OK we'll have two kids' burgers with fries and two adult burgers with fries. Sprites all around."

"I'll have your food to you as soon as possible, less than twenty minutes."

"Thank you, Alice."

While waiting for the burgers, the boys played with one of the racing video games. Jack and Becky sat in silence, looking at each other occasionally, not daring to take the chance to discuss what was going on, in case the room was bugged.

The food finally arrived, and the boys got theirs and returned to their video games, as Becky and Jack sat at the round table to eat.

"Man, I'm so hungry and tired," Becky said as she held up the disappearing ink pen, looking at Jack for a sign. Jack looked at her, and then he looked at the glass of Sprite.

He nodded and said, "If you don't mind, I just want to eat right now, and we will talk later."

"That works for me," Becky said as she started to write on the notepad that was on the table.

When Daniel and Jack started the company, they attended a Private Eye convention. They saw a lot of cool stuff, some of which they purchased and used in their day-to-day operations. However, there was a novelty booth at the convention, and as a gag, Daniel bought a bag of Disappearing-ink pens.

As you wrote on a piece of paper, the ink would disappear in about five seconds, and to make it reappear, you would place the palm of your hand directly on it for ten seconds or more. The body heat would cause the ink to appear, but after about ten seconds, the ink would disappear again.

This was a great way of passing notes, however, the only problem was that you could not erase it. So, someone later could reactivate it with body heat. By accident, Becky discovered that if you damp a paper towel in Sprite, you could erase the words and the ink would not appear again.

Becky handed Jack the piece of paper she had been writing on.

"Do you know what Mary was talking about when she said you started all of this?"

Jack read the note and wrote his response, *"There is only one case that was a little hinky, and we dropped it."*

They continued to write back and forth.

Becky wrote, *"Wait, was that the Navy Officer case? Her husband thought she was having an affair."*

Jack wrote, *"Yeah, she was in the Airforce and he was in the Army. But out of nowhere, the husband called and said to drop the case. He said for us to keep the balance of the deposit for the time used."*

After reading Jack's note, Becky thought for a moment, and wrote, *"I remember you and Daniel talked about it a couple of times on the phone. You must have said something to trigger the NSA (National Security Agency) system protocol."*

Jack shook his head as he wrote, *"We didn't do anything else, we dropped the case. What is NSA?"*

After reading Jack's question, Becky took a moment to think. She forgot Jack was not aware of some of the government surveillance. Since she and Daniel had been in the military, they were more aware than most people.

Taking a moment to organize her thoughts, Becky wrote, *"Big brother listening stuff. You must have said or done something because we know that once the NSA system is triggered, it looks for additional alerts, and if there are none, the file is archived. Jack, do you remember doing or saying anything over the phone, or by email?"*

Jack read the last note, and then he just stared at the paper for a long time. He nodded as he read about the NSA's system protocol; he remembered Daniel saying something about it, but he had not paid much attention.

Jack continued to read, after a moment his hands trembled a little, and he slowly looked up at Becky with a look of fear on his face.

Becky said out loud, "Jack, what did you do?!"

His look changed from fear to downright fright, he opened his mouth to speak but could not. Returning to the notepad, he started to write furiously.

CHAPTER THREE
RIGHT AS RAIN

It had been nearly a year ago that Jack was working as a night-shift restaurant manager. After ten years in retail management and two divorces, from the same woman, Jack found himself in restaurant management.

People asked him why he married the same woman twice. "She didn't quite clean me out the first time," he would say, "she had to practice. The second time she had it perfected." As an extra punchline, he added, "Like Richard Pryor used to say in one of his jokes, *You got any dreams, I want them too. Yes, she took everything, including my dreams.*"

The jokes were his way of hiding the fact that he still loved his ex-wife. However, anyone paying close attention could see the pain and hurt in his eyes. And yet, there was somewhat of a resolve there also, because he knew that the woman was just no damn good for him.

Having never worked in a restaurant before, Jack assumed it would be like retail, just with food, he could not have been more wrong. It was hard enough dealing with 300 to 400% employee turnover, but he was not prepared to deal with customers who were just plain nasty people.

He often thought, *"Is that how you act in your own home?"*

Working the Friday night shift, for some reason, he picked up an earworm, *"Another Saturday Night, and I ain't got nobody, I got some money 'cause I just got paid. I wish I had someone to talk to…"* It was a Friday night, but the Sam Cook song lingered in Jack's mind like a slow-moving fog.

As the weekend manager of the family-style restaurant, he was pleased as he made his way around the restaurant. The food orders moved through the window in an orderly manner, and the salad girls were on point with the salad and soup bar.

It turned out to be an easy Friday night, with a decent restaurant crowd and no major issues with service or the kitchen. Erica, the hostess/cashier on duty was well-seasoned. It was the kind of Friday night that should have made Jack happy and in good spirits.

Erica was a college student who would be graduating in a couple of months. All of the restaurant managers had discussed it and agreed to offer the Dining Room Manager position to her when she graduated.

Not only was she cute, but she was also smart, and a highly perceptive young woman. She noticed that Jack seemed to be a little jumpy.

"Are you OK? Is there something wrong?"

The question seemed to give Jack pause. For a moment he seemed to ponder the question before he shook his head no, and walked off without saying anything.

Erica's question caused Jack to ask himself, *OK, why am I so jittery tonight? I made additional rounds checking the tables, the wait staff, the kitchen, the front door, and even extra checks on the bathroom, but there was nothing out of the ordinary.* Looking at his watch, 9:00. *Just a couple more hours, almost home free.* Still, the uneasiness did not go away.

As Jack headed to the back of the dining room, the rubbing sound from the front doors caused a chill down his back. The two wooden doors at the entrance made the sound as one opened and rubbed against the other.

He turned to glance back, which was his routine. However, this time when he looked back at the doors, the sight gave him a level of anxiety he had not experienced since he was a teenager.

Standing there in his white dress Navy uniform, with his hat tucked under his left arm, was Daniel Draper. Jack and Daniel had not seen each other since Daniel left to join the Navy. The unexplained chill now ran down Jack's spine, and as he rubbed one of his forearms, he felt the hairs on his arm standing up.

Somehow Jack sensed that there was a change coming, he thought, *What the hell, I haven't seen you for fifteen years.*

Without a word, Daniel's presence spoke volumes. Standing there, his 5'10" muscular frame made him look taller. Daniel did an almost undetectable, deliberate scan of the dining room. This was more than just his training; it was a part of his personality.

Damn, he looks like he just stepped out of a Navy recruitment poster. Jack wasn't sure if he said it out loud, or just thought it.

Jack and Daniel attended different high schools in Alabama. Daniel went to a county school, and Jack went to a city school. They met while working at a local grocery store and became good friends.

The two of them couldn't be any more different. Jack was a black heavy-set city kid, and Daniel was a thin wiry white country boy, but they hit it off straight away and became best friends. Daniel was the type of loyal friend who would turn over heaven and earth to help a friend; however, if you ever made an enemy of him, he would go through hell to get at you.

Approaching Daniel with a smile and an extended hand, he said "Hey buddy!" He motioned to Erica, the hostess, that he would take care of this guest. With a mixture of surprise and confusion in his voice, he asked, "How have you been?"

After they gave each other a good firm handshake and buddy hug, Daniel said, "All is fine, right as rain."

The response gave Jack pause because that is what they used to say when they needed to talk in private. Jack had not heard that phrase for fifteen years. Showing Daniel to a table and handing him a menu, he told the server that Daniel could have whatever he wanted, and added, "The check is on me."

Leaning over so Daniel could hear, "Buddy, this is a busy time, I'm starting the process of closing the restaurant for the night. Do me a favor, take your time, and eat your meal, once I lock up in about an hour, I'll have some time to sit with you."

"OK, don't worry about it, I have nothing else to do."

As Jack walked back to the kitchen, he wondered about the response Daniel gave him. *What's going on? Why is he here after all of these years?*

Looking through the glass in the kitchen door to see how Daniel was doing, he noticed he had moved to the other side of the booth, so he was facing the front door. *Curious,* He thought. *It must be a military thing.* But then he remembered that Daniel was that way in high school. He always wanted to see who was coming in the door.

As Jack went on with preparing to shut down the restaurant for the night, he reflected on fifteen years ago, before Daniel went into the Navy.

Daniel had a girlfriend named Cindy, she worked in the office of the grocery store where Jack and Daniel worked. Everybody liked Cindy, she had a charming and innocent personality, except for how she walked.

Men and women both would turn to watch her walk whenever she walked through the store. She had this very natural sway, not contrived or make-believe, but a natural hypnotic rocking back and forth. It was indeed a pleasure watching her move grocery carts from in front of the office door to the other side of the register stands.

It was funny how many carts found their way to that office door. Thinking back, Jack figured Cindy must have known that the boys put the carts near the office door so she would have to move them.

Daniel was madly in love with Cindy, but Cindy had a secret. One Tuesday night, Daniel came to the store to tell Jack that he had joined the Navy and would ship out in two days. Jack was shocked and asked why he had not said something. All Daniel said was, "All is fine, right as rain. You will understand tomorrow." Then he just turned and left the store.

As Jack drove onto the store's parking lot on Wednesday after school, he sensed something was wrong. Walking into the store, there was a man in a suit on the pay phone outside the front doors. Jack later learned that he was the District Manager for the store.

Inside the store, a uniformed cop was standing by the office door. The Cashiers and other employees were busy looking busy, but no one was getting any work done.

Mark, a co-worker and a student with Jack at the same high school, called Jack back into the storage area and told him the whole story. With a sense of quiet and mystery, leaning in close, Mark said,

"It turns out that Cindy, Daniel's girlfriend, was having an affair with Ralph the store manager. Somehow Daniel found out and told Ralph's wife. She was in earlier while I was stocking the wall near the backside of the office, and I heard everything as she had it out with Ralph."

Now Jack understood what Daniel had been doing for the last couple of weeks when he didn't have time to hang out. He must have been following Cindy and Ralph.

Mark continued with the story, "When the District Manager got here, Ralph's wife confirmed she was the one who faxed the pictures to the district office of Cindy and Ralph coming and going from the Robert's Motel."

"Wow!" was all Jack could say.

Yes, that was all fifteen years ago. He had not seen Daniel again until tonight. After finishing the last of his paperwork, and sitting down with Daniel, Jack pointed to the remaining workers with a sly smile. "All of these clowns will be out of here in fifteen minutes, and we will have a couple of beers,"

"Y'all serve beer here?"

"One of the batter recipes calls for a premium beer, and we keep a case in the cooler. It's against the law to drink in this restaurant because we don't have a liquor license.."

True to his word, once he locked the doors behind the last employee, Jack brought out a six-pack of beer.

At first, they did some small talk, some catching up, some remembering when, and yes, they even talked a little about Cindy being the reason Daniel joined the Navy.

Finally, Daniel said, "I was asked to retire from the Navy, with honors, but still, I have to get out." Looking at Daniel, not knowing what to say or what questions to ask.

Jack joked, "What happened? You caught someone sleeping with your wife?"

Daniel smiled slightly and said, "No, my wife Becky is not like Cindy."

Since Daniel was still smiling, Jack decided to ask more about Becky. "So, she is in the Navy too?"

"No, actually, she was in the Air Force, and we met in the dining hall on base in Germany. I couldn't miss that Alabama accent when I heard her talking. After introducing myself to her, it was like we were meant to be."

"On our third date, I asked her to marry me. We've been married for eight years now. Know what the strange thing is?"

"Stranger than you asking a woman to marry you after three dates?"

With a wide grin on his face, Daniel said, "Yes, stranger than that. She is from Athens Alabama, just thirty minutes from my house."

They laughed and made jokes about Daniel going to Germany to find a wife, whose home was thirty minutes from him in Alabama. He could have gone to her house on his lunch break.

Finally, Jack said, "So, what did you do so wrong that they asked you to leave the Navy, but not wrong enough to give you a dishonorable discharge?"

Daniel's mood changed, and the light in his eyes darkened a little as he spoke, "It all has to do with a training exercise, I used the wrong amount of C-4 at the training school at Redstone while I was back for a mandatory training rotation."

"The training facilitator put the decimal point in the wrong place, and I didn't catch it. A couple of guys got hurt, but no one died, command asked that I remove myself anyway."

"If it wasn't your fault, why are they punishing you?"

"Because part of my training was to verify the specific detonation instructions and requested explosive values. They fired the facilitator because he was a contractor. One of the young men who got hurt was the son of some mucky-muck in Washington, so they wanted my head. The only way to save my pension, and good name, was to take a voluntary exit."

"Wow," Jack said with a low, slow sound, "What will you do now? What can I do to help?"

Daniel gave him that look he had not seen since they worked at the grocery store together. Whenever Daniel had an idea or was up to something, he got this look in his eyes.

"Bones, what are you up to?"

Bones is what Jack used to call Daniel when they were spending time together, and all was right with the world. The name came from when Jack brought Daniel home to meet his mom, she said, "You ain't nothing but skin and bones, I got to feed you."

She made them sit down for dinner. They had a meal of cornbread, mac & cheese, fried chicken, greens, and cherry Kool-Aid. They laughed and had a great time that night, and the name "Bones" just reminded them of that time and the warm feelings it brought.

Before Daniel started, Jack told him to hold on and got another six-pack of beer. As Jack set the new six-pack on the table, he could tell Daniel wanted to talk, and the chill down his back returned. He said nothing, just waiting for Daniel to talk.

"I'm going to use the money I have saved to open my own private investigation company." He paused, looked at Jack, and said, "I want you to come and work for me."

"What are you talking about?!" Jack yelled,

"Hear me out, will you? See, I'm a soon-to-be-retired Navy Seal, and clandestine research is what we are all about, so being a P.I. is no big deal."

The thought was not a far-fetched idea to Jack, Daniel had always had a covert nature and it was just part of his personality.

"What do I know about being a private eye? I sure don't know anything about being a Magnum P.I. or Banacek! Are you crazy?"

After more talking and completing their fourth six-pack of beer, Daniel said, "I need someone, like you, with a business background to help me run the company. I want you as a business partner, Becky was some sort of records keeper in the Airforce and can make sure the books are right and tight."

It was about two-thirty in the morning when both the beer and conversation were through, and Jack decided to join his friend in this new adventure. Mostly because he trusted Daniel and because he was so done with the restaurant business.

With a satisfied grin, Jack extracted a crisp $100 bill from his wallet and with satisfaction, and deliberate purpose, he laid the bill on top of the cluttered table. He smiled as he went to the cash register stand.

Finding an envelope, he wrote on it, "Consider this my letter of resignation, I quit." With the envelope in hand, walking through the front doors, he took a deep breath, as if he had not breathed fresh air for a while.

He locked the doors, put the restaurant keys in the envelope, and slid the envelope in through the space between the double doors. He thought, *Let the adventure begin.*

CHAPTER 4

When Jack got home from the restaurant, he cut the ringer off on his house phone, letting the answering machine catch all calls. His ranch-style home, in the quiet neighborhood, was his sanctuary.

He slept all day Saturday, until around 4:30 pm, still feeling the effect of the beer he consumed Friday night with Daniel.

The blinking numbers on his answering machine showed 24 messages, the maximum the answering machine would hold.

While the fresh pot of coffee was brewing, he pushed the play button on the answering machine. After the first three, he fast-forwarded through the rest of the messages.

He smiled he said to himself, *I didn't know I was that popular.* After pushing the "erase all" button, he poured himself a big mug of coffee.

Feeling the coffee stimulate his brain, he replayed the conversation with Daniel the night before in his mind. For the rest of the afternoon, Jack flipped channels on the T.V., but he couldn't find anything that interested him, not even on Home Box Office.

Clicking off the T.V. and slamming the remote down, he thought, *Nearly a hundred channels and there is nothing on.*

He knew the real problem. Although he was excited about starting the P.I. company with Daniel, he could not shake the feeling that there was something Daniel wasn't telling him.

In high school, Daniel had a way of not presenting the complete picture unless he had to – and Jack had the feeling there was more to the story than what he was telling him.

That evening was no better, Jack was tired and thought he would have a couple of beers and go to sleep. After drinking the last three beers in his fridge, he still couldn't get to sleep. So he jumped in his car, drove down to the corner store, and bought a twelve-pack.

After another three beers, he decided he had enough, but he still couldn't fall asleep. He could not get his mind to quiet down.

He found himself tossing and turning in the bed. He got hot, so he pushed the covers off. Then he got cold and pulled the covers on. The mattress seemed to get hard so he moved to the foot of the bed, that was no good, so he moved back to the head.

He couldn't seem to breathe, so he laid across the middle of the bed. Nothing seemed to work. Laying there in the quiet of the night, the sounds of cars going by his home seemed to be louder than normal.

As the cars drove by, their headlights would trace across the ceiling, as if tagging him.

He thought he could smell the trash in the kitchen, and considered getting up and taking it out. But he knew that would not help him get to sleep.

The last straw was when he heard a cricket outside of his bedroom window. "That's it!" He yelled as he set up on the side of the bed. Although it was 11:30 at night, he called the one person who he knew could help settle him down.

As she answered the phone, he rushed to say, "Mom, there is no emergency, no one is hurt, I just want to talk to you."

After making sure she was settled, he told her about seeing Daniel, and that he asked him to help start a detective agency. Talking for forty-five minutes, he explained his decision to quit his job, and join Daniel.

In the middle of the conversation with his mom, Jack realized that a lot of what he was feeling was fear. He was scared of failing Daniel and making a fool of himself. His mom just listened as Jack talked it out.

After listening quietly to him, she finally said, "Tell Daniel I said he is to take care of my boy and make sure you come home every night. Otherwise, I'll hurt him."

Jack chuckled, and said, "I will, Mom, and thank you for talking with me, you seem to always know what to say."

"Honey, you still haven't figured it out after all of these years. I have always been a good sounding board for you, and support you once you have made the decision."

They spoke for another couple of minutes and finally said goodnight. He felt settled and at ease enough to go to sleep. He remembered to turn the ringer to the phone on, before drifting off to sleep, he thought about what his mom said to tell Daniel.

Funny, that is what Daniel's mom used to say to Jack whenever the two boys went out. Daniel had a habit of pushing the envelope or overstepping bounds. He would often wind up in some sort of fight. Many times Jack would step in the middle of a fight to break it up, or back Daniel up because he had several guys coming at him.

After one such encounter, Jack asked, "Why do you always do that? Why do you push everything so hard and step over the line? What are you trying to prove?"

Without hesitating, Daniel said, "I'm willing to pay the cost to do what I want and to go where I want. If a man is unwilling to pay the cost, he deserves what he gets. If he listens to what everybody else tells him what he should and shouldn't do, he has no right to complain if he is pushed around."

"But Bones, a lot of time you wind up hurt, it can't be worth it."

With the sincerest answer Jack had ever heard, and with the strongest look on his face, Daniel looked at Jack and said, "I'll have a lifetime of memories of things I've done and the places I have been because I was willing to pay the price, and hell, it only hurts for a little while."

As if in a reflective thought, he added, "They say what doesn't kill you makes you stronger, I say what doesn't kill me – better hide." After that, Jack never asked him again and always backed his buddy when he needed it.

The memories of him and Daniel as teenagers were what he needed to calm his mind. Finding a comfortable position in bed, with images of the 70's T.V. detective shows like Joe Mannix, James Rockford, and Magnum P.I. dancing through his head, he entered a quiet, peaceful sleep.

The phone ringing woke Jack up early Sunday morning, It was Daniel. "I have a job for you, it is an insurance fraud case in some small town outside of Memphis."

Surprised to receive an assignment so quickly and unaware Daniel's company was already up and running, Jack asked the obvious (to him) question.

"How did you get a case already? Your official discharge is not until a week from now, I don't understand,"

"I've been planning to open this agency for quite some time. I've been working with R.R.C. Investigations. (Research, Record, and Case Investigations) is a P.I. firm I have worked for in the past. They have a job they need to do this week, and I can't get to it. They will pay you $15 an hour to do the job."

Jack agreed to contact R.R.C. Investigations and get the case file, and the necessary information. He entered the R.R.C. office at 9:00 am Monday and met with Randy Allen, the owner.

Jack and Randy sat in his office and Randy's secretary brought them both coffee. Since Randy didn't know Jack, he asked him questions about his background, how he knew Daniel, and if he thought he could do the assignment.

After they talked for about fifteen minutes, Randy gave Jack the case file for him to read. While reading the case file, Jack listened to Randy give an overview.

"The subject is a union employee at a large tire plant who is supposed to be 100% disabled. He should wear a neck brace all the time and take the highest amount of pain medication allowed for walking around.

He is supposed to hurt when he takes a breath, and we have reports he is scamming the company. We need you to go down and get some videos of his activities."

From the picture in the file, Jack saw that the subject was an African American, and figured that was the reason they wanted him for the job.

Once Jack said he would accept the assignment, Randy gave him keys to a company car with a car phone, $2000 cash, a camcorder, a map, and directions.

As Jack stood and turned to leave the office, Randy said, "Oh, did I mention, he is also a preacher, and his church is having a revival this week? That should be a great place to get some videos."

"See what you can get of him coming in and out of the church. If you can get more, that would be great."

Jack received additional instructions from Randy's secretary, the most important of which was not getting a hotel room in the town. The head of the union and the Deputy Sheriff were brothers, who would recognize R.R.C. cars. She recommended that Jack get a hotel room in an adjacent town for his safety.

The drive took just a little longer than what Jack was expecting, he barely made it to the town before that Monday night's church service started.

He found an excellent parking space in a parking lot next to the church's parking lot.

Ok, I'll get videos of the preacher entering and exiting the church. I can spend the next couple of days following him to see what other shots I can get. That should be enough to show him scamming the insurance company.

Just as Jack completed the plan in his mind, a man walked across the parking lot toward his car. He spotted the man just in time to lay his coat over the video camera. Jack could see he was checking him out very carefully. Being proactive, he called the man over to the car.

Jack quickly came up with a suitable cover story. "Sir, I'm from out of town and was eating in the Kentucky Fried Chicken a couple of blocks away, and I heard this church was having a revival."

"Yes sir, we are."

"Oh, are you a member?"

"Yes sir, I'm headed to the church now, want to come?"

Jack thought, *Note to self, learn to do covert surveillance.*

After pulling his car into a proper parking space in the church's parking lot, Jack got out and shook the man's hand.

He was so busy trying to think up a story that would allow him to take the video camera into the church, Jack forgot the man's name as soon as he said it.

Jack said, "I'm always on the road, and I carry a portable video player. Do you think I can videotape the service?" Jack held his breath as he looked the man in the face, waiting for his answer.

After giving it some thought, the man said, "Sure, why not? The Pastor would enjoy having you tape his service."

The whole thing was surreal to Jack, as he entered the church, the Pastor and his family were also entering. The church was a typical southern two-room and bathroom church. It had a red brick front, and the rest of the outside was white lap-siding, in much need of painting.

The preacher was a medium-sized man, about 5'10", and dressed in a dark gray suit. His wife was younger in appearance, and although modestly dressed, she gave much thought to how she looked.

The man with Jack stopped them and started to introduce him.

"What is your name anyway?" The man asked, Jack had not prepared a cover story with a name and background, his brother's name was the only name he could think of on the spot.

"Jimmy from Alabama."

The man introduced Pastor Davis, his wife Mother Davis, and two teenage boys Richard and Marcus. The boys were well-disciplined and very polite, but they did not want to be there.

The man continued, "Jimmy wanted to know if he could videotape your sermon so that he could watch it in the hotel room?" The Pastor smiled a big smile and said yes and showed Jack to a good spot so that he could get a good view.

All night long, Jack introduced himself as, "Jimmy from Alabama." At one point between introductions, Jack thought, *Note to self, come up with a cover name.*

During the service, it occurred to Jack, *If this preacher weren't a crook, his preaching would have been good.*

From Jack's seat in the third row in the middle of the small church, there were six or seven rows of metal folding chairs, and each row held about 10 or 11 chairs. Jack got wide shots, zoom-shots, panned the stage, and ensured he got it every time the Pastor jumped, spun, or danced.

The pastor was giving a good sermon, and there were "Amen," "Hallelujah," and other cries of affirmation from the congregation throughout the sermon.

Jack reminded himself that he was there to do a job, *This man was supposed to be in such pain that it would hurt him to breathe.*

At the end of the service, Jack went up and thanked the Pastor for the wonderful sermon, his wife for her singing, and the two boys for their instrument playing. One son played the keyboard, and the other played an electric guitar. Jack asked one more favor, "I got some great video out there, but the light here is feeble. Do you think I can get a close-up of you and your family?"

The Pastor smiled and said he could. Jack took off his glasses and laid them on a stool on the stage. He got a good close-up of the Pastor and then panned the whole family, even filming the shoes he was wearing.

"What great shots", Jack thought as he left the church, he was so proud of himself for a successful first assignment.

"Wow, I'm so hungry!" Jack exclaimed out loud. "Man, I'm as hungry as if I had worked an eight-hour shift." Pulling into the first Burger King he came to, he went inside to order because the drive-thru looked like it was backed up.

Standing in line and not being able to make out the menu items; reaching to adjust his glasses, he could not find them on his face or head. He thought for a moment, *I took them off at the church and laid them on that stool.*

How stupid is that? he asked himself while getting back into his car. As he pulled into the church's parking lot, the Pastor and his family were coming out of the church door, and the

Pastor's wife was holding his glasses in her hands. He got out of his car, leaving it running, hoping to make some funny joke, get his glasses, and be on his way.

Walking with a hurried pace, and with a big smile on his face, Jack said to the Pastor's wife. "Thank you so much. I couldn't even order food at Burger King."

As he reached for his glasses, she smiled and said, "No problem, we stayed a little longer, hoping you would make it back."

After more thankyou's, handshakes, and some joke about his memory, he hurried back to his car. As he was driving out of the church parking lot, Jack thought, *Note to self, don't take off your glasses at a surveillance location.*

Jack made his report and turned over the car, camera, the file, along with the remaining cash and his receipts from the trip, to the R.R.C. manager. The Manager had payroll cut him a check for $600. Jack was surprised, he asked why his check was so much. The Manager explained, "If you travel out of town for two days or more, we automatically pay you for 40 hours."

Jack briefed Daniel that evening, and he could hardly contain himself in recounting the whole assignment. He even told him about leaving his glasses at the church. They had a big laugh, and Daniel said he would tell Becky.

"You should enjoy the rest of the week off because next Monday we start your first day of actual training. I'll pick you up at 7 am. Your training starts right now.

When you have an appointment to meet someone or to start surveillance, you start the night before. Make sure you have whatever you're going to need and plan to be at your destination at least fifteen minutes early, thirty minutes would be better. So, you should be waiting for me outside your house Monday morning, I should not have to wait on you."

On Monday, Jack started a week-long training course, which included tailing targets, online computer research, and calling people on the phone to get information. Although Jack was already impressed with Daniel, he found the skillsets of tailing people very impressive.

However, the most impressive thing was how Daniel could drive by a driveway full of cars at 30 to 40 miles per hour and recall their tag numbers. Jack also had to learn how to use the new cell phone and home computer Daniel bought for him.

Finally, Jack started to feel a little like a Private Investigator when Daniel said, "You have some natural unrealized skills and a great bullshit detector."

Jack felt ready for whatever came his way. At least he thought he was, but he had no idea.

CHAPTER 5

Daniel completed two weeks of one-on-one training with Jack. It was Friday night of the last week of training, and Jack was at home, drinking beer and flipping TV channels.

When Daniel had dropped him off at home around 6:00 PM, he said, "Buddy, you're ready. Your training from now on will be on the job."

Around 9:30 that evening, Jack received a call from Daniel. "Make sure your fax machine is hooked up," Daniel started without saying hello or any other greeting. "So I can fax over the case file on your new assignment. That way, you can jump right on it Monday morning."

Jack said, "What, no hello or kiss my ass or nothing?"

Daniel chuckled and said, "Oh, I'm sorry. It's been a long day, and I just wanted to make sure you have the new case file. So, hello, how are you?"

Jack started to say something, but Daniel interrupted, "That's great, glad to hear it. Make sure your fax machine is on."

Jack stammered a little and said, "Okay, I guess this is it – I'm ready. What kind of case is it?"

"It is a domestic case, a woman thinks her husband is cheating on her, and wants us to get her the proof."

Daniel didn't provide any other details. He just told Jack to double-check the fax machine and then hung up the phone without saying goodbye.

In just a few moments, the fax machine rang and started making a buzzing noise. Jack retrieved the pages. Mary Woodruff was the client, she suspected her husband, Andy Woodruff, of having an affair.

As he read the fax about Andy, he learned that Andy worked for the Huntsville Police Department and was the man who took the jail prisoners out to do trash pickup on the city streets.

The revelation that Woodruff was a city cop caused Jack's neck hairs to stand up, and he got a queasy feeling in the pit of his stomach. Jack knew there was potential danger if Woodruff found out Jack was following him. After all, Woodruff had the full force and authority of the police department at his disposal.

While Jack was reading the contents of the Woodruff file, the phone rang, it was Daniel again, "Oh – I forgot to mention the last P.I. Mrs. Woodruff had on the case ended up in the hospital."

Jack heard the concern in Daniel's voice. He continued, "Make sure you are safe, and remember he can spot a sloppy tail." Before Jack could say anything, Daniel hung up.

Monday morning, Jack had no problems finding Officer Woodruff's truck because the city's ordinance required the prisoners' cleanup routes to be published in the paper the week before.

He parked down the road far enough to be out of normal sight range but close enough to see Woodruff's truck, and if anyone approached the truck.

After parking his car, Jack looked up at the sky and marveled at what a beautiful day it was. *I bet on a day like today, those men wish they did not have to go back to the jail.*

However, the sun was beaming through the front windshield. Because of the road crew's route, Jack had to park facing the morning sun. He saw a spot that would be a great location, but it was too far away.

He made a mental note to himself, *Remember to pick up binoculars and a high-power zoom lens for the camera Daniel gave me.*

That first day was uneventful. He observed the work truck at a safe distance, he watched as the crew broke for lunch, at a local café. The only person who approached the truck was the server who brought the carryout to Woodruff and the men.

They took another little break in the afternoon, about ten minutes, and then continued to work the rest of the afternoon without stopping. At about 4:30 pm, they finished and started back to the jail. The city ordinance required all prisoners to be back in jail no later than 5:15 pm.

Jack found a parking spot in the city parking garage adjacent to the police entrance to the building. He had the perfect spot, on the lower level, giving him a perfect sight line to the police's entrance and their parking lot exit.

Jack was glad that after 5:00 pm, parking was free in the city garages. The parking spot he selected was perfect, it allowed him to see which direction Woodruff would turn when he left the garage, and he could exit the parking garage based on Woodruff's turn.

He figured Woodruff had to do the paperwork to end his shift, which should take about thirty minutes or so. While waiting, Jack ticked off a checklist in his head of his lucky breaks.

The subject drives a special vehicle,

There is a predetermined route,

Great parking spot across from the police department,

A single door for officers to start and finish their shifts.

At that point, Jack stopped, asking out loud, "What kind of car does he drive?" He quickly looked through the file he had on Woodruff but could not find any mention of a car. Before, he just casually observed the police officer's exit door, but now he paid closer attention because he would have to see what kind of personal car Woodruff was driving.

After about two hours, Jack got worried, because he had not seen the subject come out. *Had he missed Woodruff, or was he still in the building?*

Finally, nearly three hours later, he spotted Woodruff exiting the building, and for someone who just worked an eight-hour shift and done three hours of paperwork, he had a little bounce in his step.

To Jack's surprise, Woodruff's whole demeanor was that of a man feeling pretty good. Jack thought, *OK, he is about to go and meet his woman.*

Woodruff got into a light green Monte Carlo, which looked to be about 1978 or 1980 model. Once Jack saw which direction the subject turned, he pulled out of the parking garage and followed him.

It was evening time, with fewer cars on the road, and he could easily be spotted. Always crossing over behind the subject's car, Jack used a parallel tail with confirmed sightings every block or so.

When they were within a mile or so of Woodruff's home, Jack sped up on a side street, he entered from the other end of Woodruff's street and parked up the block from his home. After Woodruff went into his home, Jack watched the house until 12:30 am, the lights went out at about 11:00 pm, after which there were no signs of movement.

The following day Jack reviewed the scheduled route for Woodruff, but he waited for stores to open at 10:00 am so that he could stop and buy a zoom lens and a pair of binoculars.

After making his purchase, and getting some professional pointers about the camera lens, he got on the road. Jack drove to the area where he thought they may have been. As he stopped at the stoplight, he looked to his right and saw the truck in the parking lot next to him.

They had engine trouble and had someone working under the hood. Jack continued straight and parked down the block so he could watch but remained inconspicuous. He used the time to test his new equipment, first the binoculars.

They worked great and allowed him a close-up view and the ability to identify people around the truck. Next, he attached the high-power zoom lens to the camera, Jack was blown away by how clear and close-up he could see.

He could zoom in close enough to read lips if he knew how. He could count the buttons on Woodruff's shirt; in fact, he had lost one.

As Jack played around with the camera, zooming in and out, panning from side to side, something caught his eye. In a Ford Escort, a woman parked a half-block over, she was also looking at Woodruff with a pair of binoculars. "What the hell?"

He looked in the file folder at a picture of Mrs. Woodruff, and sure enough, it was her. Jack could do nothing now; the men were getting into the truck and about to return to their route. Jack followed the routine he had followed the day before, driving ahead of the truck and parking as far away as visibility would allow.

However, he had an extra chore today, watching the woman who hired them. She was easy to spot in the Ford Escort that drove by the truck four or five times, slowing down to take a good look.

At the end of the shift, Jack followed the subject back to the police department and parked in the adjacent parking garage to observe.

He didn't see Ms. Woodruff parked down the street until Mr. Woodruff came out of the building about three hours later, she then sped off to beat him home.

Jack followed Woodruff home, parked down the road, and observed the house until about 11:30 pm. He decided to go home and give a field report early and not wait until Friday. He had to let Daniel know that Mrs. Woodruff had appeared.

Jack called Daniel but was quick to apologize for such a late call. "Buddy, I am so sorry for calling so late, but something happened today that I think you need to know about."

Daniel played off the fact that Jack woke him up. "No worries buddy, I was just getting settled for the evening. What's going on?"

Jack told him about seeing Mrs. Woodruff, while he was surveilling Mr. Woodruff.

"I was afraid of that," Daniel said, "That is how the last P.I. got spotted and was beaten up by Mr. Woodruff. He knows his wife is following him, he doesn't know we are also following him. With the other P.I., she would jockey for position in tailing Mr. Woodruff, and that is how he spotted the other P.I. I'll take care of it tomorrow."

"How will you do that?"

"I'll intercept her and tell her that if she doesn't back off, we'll drop her as a client," Daniel said with anger showing in his voice.

The next day Jack started his observation of Mr. Woodruff as he was leaving his home, taking pictures as he came out of his home and got into his car. Since Jack knew where he was going, he parked on a cross street halfway between Woodruff's house and the police department.

After taking pictures as Woodruff drove by, Jack drove right to the parking garage. He had to pay to get in at this time because it was during regular business hours. Jack parked in the same spot as before and was able to take pictures of Woodruff entering the building. Jack also got photos of Woodruff exiting the building to get in the truck and pick up the prisoners.

The day was like the others, lunch at about the same time in a different place, and a different person bringing the lunch out to the truck. That evening ended like all the others, and Woodruff took up to three hours to complete his paperwork.

Jack noticed other cops reporting for the end of their shifts, and to a man and woman, not one took more than thirty minutes to complete paperwork and leave. But Woodruff always took 2 ½ to 3 hours each day.

On that Friday, Jack decided to take a different approach. Since the subject's day was scripted, Jack decided not to follow him. Jack arrived at the police station an hour before the subject's shift started.

Watching the police building all day, he took pictures of the women who entered and left, noting the times and how they coordinated with the start and end of shifts. He was also able to see which women police officers went on patrol. Only one woman did not leave for patrol; she was a slim redhead.

At the end of the shift, Jack took pictures and noted each female cop as she entered the building and the time she left. All the women, but one, had already left the building when Woodruff ended his shift. He left the building two hours and forty minutes after entering.

This time Jack did not follow, he just sat watching the building. Ten minutes after Woodruff left, the redhead exited the building and got into her 1969 Mustang Fastback, dark blue. The personalized tag said, "FunLvn1."

"I got you now!" Jack said with a loud laugh.

He followed Ms. Fun Living 1 to her apartment complex, which had designated parking spaces for each apartment. She parked in space "203".

Instead of following Woodruff, Jack decided to follow Ms. Fun Living 1 over the weekend and on Monday. Over the weekend, she only left home to go to the grocery store and the video store. She never went out and never had any visitors.

Monday morning, Jack was parked down from the redhead's house by 6:00 am. When she came skipping out at seventhirty, he took pictures, and he was able to take a close-up shot of the smile she had on her face.

He followed her until they were about halfway to the police station. He took a parallel street to the city garage, but there was a car in his place this time, and the whole lower level was full.

There must be something special going on today. He thought to himself. He had to park on the second level, facing the wrong direction. At the risk of being seen, Jack got out of his car. He rushed to the corner of the garage facing the police station, just in time to see the redhead get out of her fastback and enter the building. He could only get pictures of her back as she entered the building.

Going back to his car, he kept watch on the parking spaces near the police station. Jack quickly moved his car to the spot, once he saw the car parked there leave.

Staying by the building all day, at the end of the day's shift, he took pictures of all the women leaving the building. Once again, the redhead was the only one still in the building.

Woodruff entered the building at the end of his shift and did not come out until nearly three hours later. Jack took pictures of him leaving, and about ten minutes later, the redhead came out, Jack tailed her all the way home.

Jack called Daniel and said, "I got her. I know who the other woman is." He explained how he figured it out and how he would now focus on getting the proof.

Daniel gave him a that-a-boy and said, "See, I told you that you are a natural. Let me know if I can help you. Oh, have you seen the wife lately?" Jack told him no and asked whether he took care of it, and Daniel said he did.

That night, Jack used the online reverse lookup and input the redhead's address. Sure enough, a name appeared, "Rachael Funderburk." He was able to input the name and get a phone number. The following day, just before she usually left the apartment for work, Jack used a phone booth down the street and called her.

"Hello," she said, sounding rushed, just what Jack wanted.

"Hello, are you the Rachael who is a police officer?" Jack asked with a bit of an uptick in his voice to sound more social.

"No, I work as a dispatcher, but I'm not a police officer."

Jack said, "I'm sorry, I have the wrong Rachael."

"No problem," she said as she hung up the phone.

Jack went directly to the parking garage and noted Rachael's arrival time. Woodruff showed up at his usual time and started his shift. As usual, Jack sat and monitored the people coming and going.

Around lunchtime, he found a phone booth and called Daniel. "Yes, her name is Rachael Funderburk, and she is a dispatcher at the police department."

Daniel said, "Great, I'll check with Mrs. Woodruff to see if she knows her."

Jack returned to his parking spot and waited till the change of shift. The night shift started rolling in, and the day shift came in to complete their paperwork. As it had started to rain hard, people arriving ran for the door, and the ones leaving ran to their cars.

The hard rain slowed to a sprinkle, and then he saw her. It was Mrs. Woodruff, parked on the street, outside of the police parking lot. "What is she doing here?" Jack asked out loud as if someone else was with him.

She stayed in her car until she saw Mr. Woodruff's work truck pull into the lot. Then she got out of her vehicle, with an umbrella in hand, and ran toward him, yelling. Jack was too far away to hear anything, but he could see from the redness of her face, and the loud tone coming from her direction that she was mad.

Officers were coming and going as the two stood in the parking lot, barking at each other. Then suddenly, WHACK, WHACK, WHACK … she started hitting him with the umbrella, all about his head and shoulders. Woodruff did his best to block the hits, Jack could only imagine how hard it must have been for him to control his urge to punch her.

He pushed her off and went into the building, officers at the door, who had been watching, prevented her from following him. This was the most exciting thing Jack had seen so far on the job.

That evening Jack did not follow anyone, he went home to figure out a way to get into the police department, so that he could see the layout – without being arrested. He ate an early dinner and hit the sack.

The next morning, he received a call from Daniel, "Are you ready for this?"

"What?"

"It appears several of the police days shift people went to Angie's last night, the bar a couple of blocks from the police department, for some drinks and finger foods, and…"

Jack sighed heavily and said, "Oh no, I missed it. If I had not gone home early, I could have gotten the shot."

"Don't worry about it, buddy, we are off the case."

"What do you mean, just because I didn't get the shot?"

Daniel took a deep breath, "No because our client got arrested late last night."

"Because of her beating him with an umbrella?" Jack asked,

"What umbrella?!" Daniel shouted.

Jack told Daniel about the umbrella beating at the end of the previous day's shift.

"Oh," Daniel laughed, "That must have happened after I called and asked Mrs. Woodruff about Rachael Funderburk. She was furious, she said she thought Rachael was her friend."

Daniel laid out the events that led to Mrs. Woodruff's arrest. "According to the bystanders, many of the day shift cops met at Angie's, the bar just a few blocks away from the police station."

"Woodruff and Rachael sat at a table with another couple. After they had been in the bar for about an hour, Mrs. Woodruff came in yelling at Mr. Woodruff, and at some point, she jumped on the table and kicked him in the face."

"That is when Rachael ran out and got in her car, it was a lovely night, and Rachael had left her driver's window down."

"While Rachael was trying to start her car, Mrs. Woodruff ran – dove halfway into the vehicle, grabbed the car ashtray, and started beating Rachael. When the crowd got to her, she was pulling Rachael through the window. That is when she got arrested."

After Jack heard the story, in shock he asked, "How do you know all of this?"

Daniel laughed and said, "She had to call me to bring bail money, and you better believe I got our payment tonight before I told her that we quit."

After a little laugh, Daniel said, "Buddy, enjoy your weekend, there are a couple of cases to start on Monday. But nothing as exciting as the wife beating the husband with an umbrella though."

After hanging up with Daniel, Jack had five beers, watched some Home Box Office, and fell into bed. After all, his weekend was free.

***

Saturday morning, around 11:00 am, Daniel's phone rang.

"Hello," Daniel answered.

"Hey buddy," It was Jack, "I got my new cellular phone, and you are my first call."

"Glad you called," Daniel said with excitement in his voice. "I have been calling your home, I was hoping you didn't go fishing. Your new cellular phone is paying for itself already."

"We have two cases that we must start today, one is an insurance case, and I must leave tonight headed for Texas."

"The other is a domestic case, you must meet with the husband tonight because the wife is out of town and will be back tomorrow. I'll fax you the information I have gathered so far."

"Oh yeah," Daniel said slowly, "And you have one more thing to do Monday on the Woodruff case."

"What do you mean?" Jack said, "I thought we were off of the case."

Daniel explained, "Mrs. Woodruff's Attorney wanted us to serve Mr. Woodruff with court papers by the end of the day on Monday. He is trying to get the divorce and child custody case in front of a judge before the pending assault case against Mrs. Woodruff gets to court."

"She is seeking full custody of their two kids, and her chances of success decrease after she has to go to court for the assault case."

Daniel faxed over the new client's contact information, and Jack called to set up a meeting for that evening. The client, Mr. John Terry, asked that they meet at an all-night diner around eleven o'clock.

As Daniel had taught him, Jack arrived at the diner at 10:30 pm. He could hear Daniel's words. "If you show up less than thirty minutes before time, you are late and possibly dead..."

When Mr. Terry walked in, Jack recognized him based on what he said he would be wearing. However, he had failed to mention that he was a military man, based on his military-style haircut and how he entered the building. Shaking hands, Jack introduced himself. "I'm Jack Campbell, you can just call me Jack."

"Thank you for meeting me so late Jack. You already know I'm John Terry, you can call me John."

"Would you like some coffee, John?'

"No thank you, I just wanted to get this meeting over with and get home. I must get up in about four hours."

Jack learned that Mr. Terry was a Captain in the Army, and his wife Denise was a Captain in the Air Force. Neither of them had seen combat, they worked in their respective service branches in some areas of intelligence. That is how they met five years ago when both attended an intra-branch conference on information and better cross-service communications.

They spent the next forty-five minutes discussing what caused Mr. Terry's concerns. He provided Jack with all the particulars related to his wife's movements, such as where she worked, her schedule, and the make and model of her car.

"Oh, yeah, her office building is on the military post about a mile from mine. if you ever have to come on the post, give the MPs this information so they can issue you a pass." He handed Jack a card with his name, rank, office building, room number, and phone number.

Looking at the card, Jack asks, "I have to give this information every time?"

"Yes, otherwise, you will not be able to get on the base, and if it is before or after work hours, they will call me at home and ask for permission to let you on."

Monday morning, Jack went by the Attorney's office and picked up the court papers he was to serve on Mr. Woodruff. The Attorney gave general instructions about which color paper goes to the person being served, to do it in a public place, and not to get into a confrontation.

Jack found Officer Woodruff stopped for a lunch break. He pulled into a parking spot not too far from the truck. Officer Woodruff was sitting in the truck's cab, with the door open as he watched the men. Jack aligned himself in Officer Woodruff's sight at a distance, so he could see him approaching and see he was not a threat.

Once he got within voice range, without shouting, he said, "Officer Woodruff, my name is Jack Campbell, and I have some papers for you. May I approach?"

Officer Woodruff stood up, more like he unfolded out of the truck. This was the first time Jack had seen him up close. The large four-door crew truck hid the fact that Woodruff was about 6'2", 250 to 260lbs.

Damn, you are big. Jack thought to himself, as he gave new thought to the course of action he had selected.

Woodruff motioned for Jack to come forward, as Jack got closer, he could see the nasty bruise on his face from where his wife had kicked him. Jack handed the folded paper to him and said,

"Officer Woodruff, you have been served." Jack could see the rage building in his eyes as he asked, "What the hell for?"

"I'm only the process server and here to deliver the paperwork," Jack said as he backed off slowly, keeping his eyes on Woodruff. But then he stopped. Jack felt a little sorry for him. The whole time he had followed this guy, he never saw him do anything bad other than have an affair. And based on his wife's behavior, Jack could understand it a little.

Jack had started to turn away, but stopped, and turned back to Woodruff, who was still reading the paper, with a scowl on his face.

In a quiet voice, Jack said, "May I offer you some information that might be of help?"

Woodruff just slowly nodded.

"Your wife is filing for divorce and is going for full custody of your kids. She and her Attorney are trying to get your divorce and child custody case in front of a judge before her assault case reaches court.

Because her chances of full custody go down the drain after that. I never had this conversation with you since I work for her Attorney, agreed?"

Woodruff nodded.

"First, tell your attorney what I just told you, and to use whatever tricks he can to get your divorce case pushed out beyond your wife's court appearance for assault. Second, have your Attorney request pictures from any surveillance done on you."

"The photos will show that you were having an affair. However, it will also show the day your wife walked up to you in the police parking lot and started whaling on you with the umbrella."

"Why are you doing this?" Woodruff asked.

"Never once did I see the temper in you, as I have seen in your wife."

Officer Woodruff reached into his shirt pocket and pulled out one of his business cards. He turned it over and wrote the words, *"One Time Use."* He handed the card to Jack and said, "This is a one-time use card, and you do not want to waste it.

Jack asked, "What do you mean one-time use?"

Woodruff gave him a stern look and said, "Life has a way of dropping crap into your lap and daring you to move. If one day that happens, this is your get-out-of-hell-free card."

"I'll use whatever available resources to put you in a better position, which may not be a cure, but it may be enough time to allow you to duck. I'll do it if you call me for something crappy like a speeding ticket, but your get-out-of-hell-free card is gone. Understand?"

Jack said he did and walked away, putting the card in his wallet behind the secret compartment flap.

Woodruff did as Jack had advised; his tip to Woodruff made a whole world of difference. The appendices and amendments to the divorce filings his attorney made put him in a better financial position. Because of the criminal case for Mrs. Woodruff, he did get joint custody too.

Mr. Woodruff also agreed to take the evening shift desk sergeant's job that was open. Not only did it mean more time with his kids, but there was also an additional $5,000 a year increase in pay.

After a couple of months, Woodruff forgot all about Jack and the "Get out of Hell-free" card. Until that night.

CHAPTER SIX

John & Denise Terry

(Enter Mary Rogers)

Denise Terry was excited because her fifth wedding anniversary was coming up next month, and she wanted to do something unique and surprising for her husband John. Her personal checking account was running low, so she decided she'd dip into their joint account, used to manage their household expenses.

She checked the balance and was surprised to see they were down to their last $1,500. She called the bank and reviewed the payments with the teller. All the checks made sense until they got to the last one.

Reading from her computer screen, the teller said, "This is the last one, check number 3514, for $1,000, paid to Draper and Associates Investigations."

"What was that for?" Denise asked the teller.

"I don't know," said the Teller, "you need to ask Mr. Terry. The check cleared about a week ago."

Denise went to the bank and picked up a copy of the check. Sure enough, it was John's handwriting and signature. She went home and started dinner, but her heart was not in it. All she could think about was the check and what John had to say about it.

John got home at about 5:50 pm, his regular time, and yelled his customary, "Honey, I'm home!" as he entered the door. He put his keys on the hallway table near the front door and sat his briefcase by the doorway that led into the bedroom. He walked into the kitchen, where Denise had the salad sitting on the kitchen island.

She had prepared spaghetti because it required very little mental concentration. As Denise put the spaghetti on the plates, John came around the island to kiss her. She presented her left cheek for his kiss.

As they sat down to eat, John realized that Denise had not said anything since he entered the home and that he had done all the talking. So, he paused on his second fork-spin of spaghetti and looked at her. "Honey, what's wrong? Why are you not talking to me?'

In a low, controlled, monotone voice, Denise said, "I was very excited about our fifth wedding anniversary and wanted to get you a special gift. So, I checked on the balance in the joint checking account." Still, in a monotone, but with a little less control, she said, "To my surprise, I found out that you wrote a check to Draper and Associates Investigations for $1,000. What in the world was that for? Why did you pay them $1,000?"

John sat there with a look of being found out on his face and tried to think of what he was going to say but couldn't find the words. Instead, he started crying and finally explained the check.

"I know you are having an affair. I was driving by Sam's Club and saw you in some man's truck pulling out of the parking lot. You were headed in the opposite direction, by the time I turned around, you were gone."

The longer John talked, the more Denise's expressions changed, moving from anger, to hurt, then to surprise. As John explained how he hired the Private Investigators, Draper and Associates Investigations to follow her, her facial expression turned to downright fear.

Seeing the fear on her face, John thought it was because she had been caught, and she feared divorce.

John touched her arms, giving them a gentle rub, he said, "Honey, whatever went wrong, we can fix it and get through this together."

With fear still present on her face, she finally spoke. "You don't understand, my concern now is for our safety," With a very serious look on her face, she said, "I have to go somewhere, while I'm gone, please don't answer the phone, and don't call anybody or go anywhere."

"What are you talking about? Where are you going? What do you mean about me not answering the phone?"

Holding his face between her hands, she looked at him, smiled slightly, and said, "You big dummy, I'm not having an affair. I hope to be able to explain when I get back, don't answer the phone!" And with that, she grabbed her shoulder bag and keys and was out the door.

John waited for two hours. He felt restless and picked up the phone several times to call one of her friends but thought better of it. He picked up his keys several times to go out and look for her but threw them back onto the table with an 'ugh.' Cutting on the T.V. to find a distraction, only then to cut it off after just a few minutes, slinging the remote across the room. He cleaned the kitchen, put the spaghetti and salad into containers, and put them into the refrigerator.

Finally, John heard Denise's car turn into the driveway. Her car made a peculiar ping when it turned into the driveway, he kept meaning to check it out. Still, for tonight John was glad to hear the ping.

He looked out the front bay window and saw her getting out of her car. It was now a little past eight o'clock pm. There was a good moonlight, however, even with the moon and the streetlights, John could not tell who had pulled in behind her in the black S.U.V. He could tell the S.U.V. had government plates on the front.

The S.U.V. had a driver who never got out of the car, but a woman in a dark business pantsuit got out of the rear passenger side and walked over to Denise. They were standing at the back passenger end of her car. They stood there talking for a few moments, neither one looked toward the house or the window where John was standing.

After what seemed like a long time, but was less than three minutes, the mystery woman reached into her right front pants pocket. She pulled out a cell phone, which was a government-issued Blackberry. After talking to whoever called for thirty seconds or less, she nodded at Denise, and they both started toward the front door.

John opened the door, the porch light was already on from when he turned it on earlier. As Denise entered the door, she stood to the side and said, "John, this is Mary Rogers, with the State Department, and Mary, this is my husband John."

After shaking John's hand, Mary pushed past him and said, "Please join us in the living room." As John and Denise sat on the sofa, Mary made a little more space between the coffee table and the sofa, and she sat on the coffee table in front of them.

Mary said, "John, although you have top-secret clearance, I had to request to clear you for S.C.I. communications, Sensitive Compartmented Information. The authorization came through while we were standing in the driveway."

John sat there looking back and forth between Denise and Mary. He was shocked and did not know what to do or say.

Mary said, "John, as you know, as part of your Security Clearance, subject to 18 U.S. Code § 798. Disclosure of classified information, you signed an N.D.A. (Non-Disclosure Agreement), which is always enforced." John nodded in agreement with Mary's statement.

"Well, Denise is under the same agreement," Mary continues, "and she could not tell you about the top-secret operation she has been part of for the past several months." At that time, Mary reached inside her left jacket pocket and pulled out a letter-size paper, folded in half, length-wise.

She opened the paper and handed it to John with a pen, "This is an S.C.I. / N.D.A. for you to sign. Once you sign it, I'll read you in on the operation."

John signed the form, handed the pen and paper back to Mary, and said, "OK, tell me what the hell is going on, and why is my wife in cars with strange men?"

Mary took the paper, folded it back up, and placed it in her left jacket pocket. She reached into her inside right jacket pocket and pulled out a copy of the check John had written to Draper and Associates Investigations. Handing it to John, "Have they started their investigations or produced any reports to you?"

Looking at the copy of the check, John said with a curious look on his face, "No, I don't know if they have had any time to do anything yet. What is this about?"

"Good, I need you to call your contact and stop the investigations, tell them you made a mistake and will pay for any work done, but be clear they are to cancel your file."

"OK, I can call tomorrow…"

Mary interrupted, "No, you need to call and stop it tonight. Can't you contact them?"

"Well," John said slowly, "I do have Draper's cell phone number for 24-hour access, I can call him on that."

"Excellent!" Mary exclaimed, "Call him now."

John called Daniel Draper and told him that he wanted to cancel the investigation. "I made a mistake, my wife is not having an affair. I'm so sorry for wasting your time. I'll of course pay you for the work you've done thus far."

Daniel, with a little surprise in his voice, "We have not done enough to spend the $1000 deposit. We will send you a refund."

"No, keep it for the trouble I caused."

After they said goodbye, John sat back on the sofa and said, "Done, now you two tell me what in the hell is going on."

Mary stood up and moved to the stuffed chair near the right end of the sofa. She took a deep breath, gave a relaxing sigh, and said, "Please do not interrupt me or ask any questions until I'm through. Do you understand?" John nodded his head in agreement and looked to his left at Denise.

Denise gave him a little smile and said, "It is OK, you'll see."

Mary started her story, which began six months prior. She explained that Denise had reached out to her immediate supervisor because of unusual contact with someone interested in her work assignment.

Mary explained, "As you know, Denise is a Captain in the Air Force, and her job description is that of Materials Operations and Compliance. The description for this job states she is to ensure that all the Air Force's materials meet specs and tolerance requirements."

"Now, this is tedious work, especially on paper, and people don't usually engage in conversation regarding her job assignment. Instead, most people would rather take an old toothbrush and scrub a B-52 airplane. But that is the idea, to bring as little attention to this position as possible, and to allow her full access to all areas, even those not directly Air Force related."

John looked at Denise and smiled because he knew how dull and unexciting Denise's job was and had often joked about finding her a better job watching paint dry. He looked back at Mary and saw that her facial expressions had changed. She now had an icy and official look as she continued.

"Most people don't know Denise's position is a liaison position with the State Department. Her mission is to track weapons technology and to ensure they are not being sold to, transferred to, or otherwise fall into the hands of unfriendly nations."

"Because of her job classification, she can redirect weapons as an urgent matter without Command, White House, or Congressional approval."

At that, John said, "Wow," and sat with his mouth open, looking at Denise for a few seconds.

Mary continued, "Denise is also in charge of a very top-secret program. Her department runs software that helps identify potential foreign operatives in the Military and civilian agencies. This software is unknown throughout the government, and only myself, my boss, and the Joint Chiefs know of its existence."

But that was just the beginning of the story. Next, Mary explained the specialized security training Denise had to go through, which allowed her to recognize when someone was too interested in her position. It was not the type of position military-type persons would come seeking to understand.

Mary spent the next hour laying out the events that led to this moment. She explained that six months ago, a former Air Force Captain, now a civilian contractor for the Air Force, met Denise Terry at the base P.X.

He was charming and nice-looking, however, when Denise mentioned her assigned duties, he paid no attention, which is the desired result, with one or two exceptions. Mary asked Denise to explain.

"You see, females in the Military are used to guys coming up to them, and they usually start with, What's your M.O.S.? Where are you from? How about a beer? When I say my M.O.S. is Materials Operations and Compliance, the next question is, What is that? Or What do you do?"

"Eugene… Eugene J Bullard, never once asked me about my job or why I did it. Because of my training, this raised a yellow flag. Also, he did not seem to see the irony of his name as an Air Force contractor." Since John had an inquiring look regarding Eugene's name, Denise elaborated.

"Eugene James Bullard was the first African-American military pilot. Bullard, who flew for France, was one of the few black combat pilots during World War I."

"Of course, every Air Force Airman knows that name, so to have the name Eugene J Bullard, for a white man, would be an interesting talking point. But he never gave it any weight, as if he didn't know the history."

Mary takes over again, "So you see, we have two yellow flags on the field: 1) Not asking anything about Denise's job, and 2) Not recognizing the historical significance of his name."

"I'm Denise's State Department Handler, she reached out to me as a point of caution. I did a level one background check on Bullard and found that his records were in order. However, nowhere in his records was there any mention of his name or that any officer mentioned it."

"That prompted me to run a level three background, which required the approval of a General. Once I laid out the facts as they were known, a General signed off on the search. That is when we found the patchwork of civilian and military records, his name only appeared in private records ten years before he entered the Air

Force. As you know, military background checks go back ten years."

"After that, his promotions were above average once in the Military and appeared to be a systematic movement through the ranks."

Once he became a Captain, his progression through the ranks just stopped. As a Captain in the Air Force, our best guess is that he had the most flexibility and mobility through all military branches. In addition, he was a high enough ranking officer to get into some restricted areas and be involved in more senior Command officers' conversations."

"We figured we had a spy on our hands, we also surmised that he is part of a network of Espionage Agents, holding ranks throughout Our Government." Mary explained that only someone with secret knowledge could know about Denise's job.

Denise took the lead in the conversation at this point. "Just so I'm clear, there has not been any sexual activity with Eugene. The only physical contact we had was a kiss on the cheek when I was getting in and out of his truck, that way, we looked like a couple."

John nodded as a sign of understanding, remembering not to interrupt. Mary continued with the story. "Command decided that we needed to get close to Eugene and see if we could uncover the network."

"Since he was reaching out to Denise, she was the best source of contact. For weeks she played along, allowing him to continue to approach her, and one day he started probing her to find her weakness."

"The day we felt the timing was right, Denise did not follow her routine and made sure she was just a little distant from everyone. We used the well-documented fact that the two of you could not have kids and are exploring the idea of IVF. The cost was prohibited, and the military insurance would not cover it. So, Denise, take over from here."

Denise took a deep breath, "Well when I allowed him to find me, I was friendly and polite, I seemed distracted. For the next few days, it was the same thing, I was not all there, and finally, he asked what was wrong. I would say it was a personal issue and change the subject. In my counter-espionage training, I learned the art of drawing someone in without exerting pressure."

"After that, each time we saw each other, I would put on what seemed like a forced, happy face. He kept asking me what was wrong. Finally, I broke down and told him. I told him I was sad because we could not have children and wanted to try IVF."

"But, the cost was tens of thousands of dollars, and our insurance wouldn't cover it. I then told him we tried to get a loan from the bank, but we did not have enough equity in our home to get 20, 30, possibly up to $50,000 needed if the process didn't work right away."

Denise and Mary alternated with the rest of the story, describing how Denise lured Eugene without appearing to do so. How each day Denise would open just a little more to Eugene.

Denise even floated the idea to Eugene of leaving the Air Force and getting a civilian job with better healthcare. She told him that she had gotten information about resigning her commission and leaving the Air Force.

On the day the hook was set, she sat by herself, reading a stack of papers. When Eugene approached her, she put on an act like trying to hide the documents from him, but he saw them and asked about them.

Denise spent several minutes rubbing her eyes, so it would look like she'd been crying when Eugene approached. However, she finally gave in and showed the papers to him.

After seeing the papers, with shock and disappointment in his voice, Eugene asked, "Are you going to resign your commission?"

"With a slight tremble in my voice, I said, 'I don't know what else to do, we want to have kids, and we want them before we are too old to enjoy them.'"

"At that, I started to cry, pretending I was trying to hold it back. I said, 'If it means I have to leave the Air Force to get the money, then that is what I'll do.'"

Mary said, "Eugene made his first direct move to recruiting her, and he asked what kind of costs were involved. Denise knew this was the first of many probing inquiries, so she responded to the question as if it were a throwaway question. She told him that if the first round worked, it would be as little as 20 to $25,000.00, but if it takes several tries, the cost could run close to $75,000."

Daily, Eugene would ask if she had decided to leave the Air Force. She would say, "No, the papers are still in my purse." Until one day, upon instructions from me, she yelled at Eugene.

Denise picked up the conversation again. "I yelled, 'No, I have not! John doesn't want me to quit. I'm not sure if he even wants a child. This is so stressful, it wasn't for the concern for the money, then I could focus!'"

"I left it at that and rushed away. The next day Eugene said, 'I have only one question for you today, are you ready?'

"I said, 'You're not going to ask me what I'm going to do again are you?'"

"No," Then he said in a quiet voice, "Suppose I could assist you in getting $75,000?"

"I almost smiled, but stopped, 'How can you do that? Do you have that kind of money?' I tried to look puzzled."

"Eugene said, 'No, I don't. If I had it, I would let you have it.' He asked me to meet just inside the doors at Sam's Club that evening, and he would explain everything."

"I put up the amount of resistance I thought appropriate, even joking that I would not rob a bank. Eugene laughed and reached out, patting me on the shoulder, and, saying, "No bank robbery, you are so funny.'"

Denise continued with the story, telling how she asked if she could bring her husband. Eugene had said not to the first meeting.

Both Denise and Mary walked John through the next few weeks of Denise's meetings with Eugene. The Sam's Club rendezvous, the truck rides, and the first time Eugene handed Denise an envelope full of money.

Denise explained how it happened. "Once we were in the truck, Eugene reached into the glove department and pulled out a white envelope. He handed the envelope to me and said, 'Open it.' I opened the envelope, and I was surprised that there was a stack of money in it. I asked how much is in here?"

"Eugene laughed and said, 'There is only $1,000 there, and every time we meet, you will receive an envelope with $1,000. That is so you can see the benefits of working with my friend, and you will not doubt the $75,000.'"

"Eugene did tell me not to create complications in our lives over the cash. He suggested that we not deposit this money into our bank accounts. He said it would be best to get a safety deposit box to keep it in."

"This is when he tried setting the hook for the first time. He said, 'You might think twice about telling your husband about the money for now. Having undocumented cash on hand could jeopardize your and his security clearances.'"

"And there was the hook trap, the only question was who was hooked?"

"The whole time Eugene was talking, he allowed me to hold the envelope of cash. He said, 'My friend will ask you for a small favor, however, the favor could violate your security oath.'"

"'So, this is the decision you must make at this moment. Do you want to do the favor?' I reached for the door handle while looking at the cash in my left hand the whole time."

"I said, 'I think I want to hear a little more about what your friend wants from me.' I then put the cash envelope in my purse, looked back at Eugene, and said, OK, what's next?"

Now John was staring as if he was a second grader sitting in the reading circle, and the teacher was reading his favorite book. At that time Mary took over the story again.

"Finally, Eugene told Denise that his friend owned a Government Contracting firm, and he needed something that was in overstock but recently went on the restricted access list."

Denise said, "so I asked, Well, what is it?"

"He said it was the Dynamic Frequency Divider Active Loop Filter Phase detector. He said he needed it to meet his deadlines."

Denise and Mary both tried to explain to John what the **D**ynamic **F**requency **D**ivider **A**ctive **L**oop **F**ilter **P**hase **D**etector was, and how it had gone on the restricted list.

This device had been an allowable military item that could be sold to foreign governments. However, as it turns out, it contained parts that were excellent substitutes for a component in the new Directed-energy Weapon. Once it was discovered, the D.F.D.A.L.F.P.D. went on to the restricted list.

Eugene's first statement regarding what his friend wanted was a misdirection. After Eugene allowed Denise a few minutes to play dumb about what he was asking for, he came clean regarding her actual duties.

"Your position is a liaison position with the State Department. You can redirect technology as an urgent matter without Command, White House, or Congressional approval. Furthermore, if the company to receive the requested item is already on the government-approved vendor list, you only have to show proper cause for the override."

Denise told John that they agreed to meet every Thursday after work at the local Sam's Club. She said that Eugene explained that she would not see him anymore on base because they should not be seen together.

The next day, Denise reported everything to Mary Rogers. She turned the money over to Mary to be noted in the security log. Somebody recorded the serial number of each bill.

Mary continued explaining, "During the next several meetings, Eugene and Denise would drive out of the parking lot and would drive around and talk. Eugene told Denise it was not easy for someone to monitor them if they kept moving. It was the same routine every Thursday until two weeks ago."

Denise explained, "On our last meeting, when we returned to the back parking lot of Sam's Club, Eugene said he saw the same car in the back of the store that was in front of the store when they left. Eugene told Denise he would reach out to her when he had checked it out."

Mary took up the narrative again, "When Denise asked when she would meet Eugene's friend, each time he said, 'maybe next meeting, I'll let you know'. It became more evident Eugene's interest was in another area."

"At the last meeting, two weeks ago, he asked about a particular software program Denise worked with as part of her daily duties. This was problematic because this software is Top-Top Secret, not even her superiors know how it works."

"We hoped Eugene would show more of his hand at the next meeting. But we have not heard from or seen him for two weeks. It seems strange for him not to make contact at all this week. We are just waiting for him to contact Denise."

John grabbed Denise and hugged her very tight; almost in tears he said, "I'm so sorry I thought you were having an affair, and the whole time you were just doing your job."

He stops and thinks for a moment. Now he has a look of fear on his face, as he turns to Mary he asks, "Did hiring the private investigators put her life in danger?"

CHAPTER SEVEN

Off The Case

(The Brandon Street Building)

Jack met John Terry in the diner, and he got all the information about his wife Denise. At 6:30 am, Tuesday morning, Jack started tailing Mrs. Terry as she left home to head to work. He followed her until she was about a mile from the entrance to the military base.

Jack had scouted the area on Monday, so he knew the best place to drop the tail, and still observe her entering the base.

He also knew the best place to pick her up, once she left the military base. A mile outside the base was a convenience store with an oversized parking lot. There were no turnoffs between the base and the store, and the area was all flat land, the store had the perfect vantage point.

"For the next two weeks, Mrs. Terry's routine remained the same, leaving for work at 6:30 am, and entering the base at 7:00 am. She would exit the military base at 3:00 pm every afternoon and head home. It was the same every day – except on Thursdays.

On Thursdays, after work, she would stop at Sam's Club, and spend three hours or more in the store. The odd thing was that she would only have a small bag of items when she left the store.

Each Thursday, Jack wondered, *What could she be doing for three hours?*

Jack thought about Woodruff, and how his girlfriend worked at the police station, so he would spend up to three hours after his shift at the station. *So, is this another Woodruff thing, is she meeting her boyfriend in the store?*

Jack reported his suspicions to Daniel, and Daniel told him, "Dude, you have to go inside to see who she is meeting."

"Yeah, I know but I don't have a Sam's Club membership. Do you?'

"No, I don't. Tell you what, you have to get a membership, make it a business membership, and we'll charge the membership as an expense to the client."

On Saturday, Jack entered Sam's Club for the first time and obtained a business membership. As he entered the store, his senses were pushed to the point of anxiety. The sights, sounds, and smells were almost overwhelming. As large as the place was, there seemed to be someone in every square foot of the building.

After completing the membership application process, and receiving two membership cards, he walked around the store to get a feel for the layout.

He intended to walk through the store, just to get a layout; but with every step, his attention was captured by something new. He had never seen the amount of free food samples in such quantities given out before. Every twenty feet or so, someone was offering free samples.

After he tried the cheese, pizza, sandwich meat, broccoli dipped in some sort of sauce, and the smoked sausage, he felt tired, and he still had two-thirds of the store to check out.

Although tempted to do some shopping, he reminded himself that he was on a job. *After all, what would I do with a gallon of mayonnaise?* After walking the floor, he ended his tour with a visit to the café at the front of the store.

This is the perfect spot, I can see the front doors, and watch the people entering from here.

No wonder they give you the free samples, you need the energy to walk through a place this big. He thought, but as he entered the café, the smells and sounds made him hungry.

Well, since I am here, I might as well get one of those hotdogs people carry on about. After getting to his car, he tried the hotdog. "Wow!" He yelled, "That is damn good."

That next Thursday, Jack was in the Sam's Club café watching the front doors. He was surprised by three things. One was the number of people entering the front doors every thirty minutes.

The second was how many people stopped in the café, some as they entered the store, and others as they were leaving.

But the one thing that surprised, and frustrated him, was that everyone was so friendly and wanted to talk to him.

He Suspected Denise Terry was meeting someone there, and not knowing who, it would be a very bad idea to get involved in a conversation with the man, or one of his friends.

Jack adjusted how he was sitting so he did not present a friendly, inviting presence. It worked; people stopped talking to him.

Looking at his watch, *Mrs. Terry should be showing up soon.* He scanned the people around him in the café, near the front doors, and anyone standing alone.

He spotted a military-looking man, based on the haircut, standing away from the front doors but in a direct line of sight, and the man kept checking his watch.

Because of his stance, Jack figured him to be some sort of officer. The man looked to be a few years younger than Mrs. Terry. He also stood out because he was not looking at any store items and stayed within sight of the front doors.

86

Got you - you sneaky bastard, Jack thought as he got up from his table and tossed his trash into the nearby waste can. He walked to an area near the front of the store allowing him to watch the door and the mystery man.

Sure enough, Mrs. Terry showed up and went directly to the man. They did not kiss, hug, shake hands, or touch in any manner. They only acknowledged each other with a smile and a gentle nod. Then they started walking together toward the back of the store, never really talking to each other.

They walked right into the Tires Center and headed straight for the store's tire center exit door.

Jack got to the exit in time to see them pulling off in a Ford F150 pickup truck, dark blue. He could not see the truck's tag, but he saw Mrs. Terry on the passenger's side.

"The game is a-foot." He said, quoting his favorite phrase from the Sherlock Holmes movies.

He had about three hours before the man and Mrs. Terry would return, so he walked around the store for about an hour. He bought some excellent night-vision binoculars because the ones he purchased for the Woodruff case did not have night-vision capabilities.

As he got into his car, Jack thought, *This man is way too careful, seems like a bit much for an affair – he is truly next level. Damn, I forgot to get a hotdog, well next time.*

He drove his car to the rear of the store and parked facing the Tires Center so he could have a good view of the truck and its driver. *I'm a little exposed here,* he thought, *but I should be ok, they don't know who I am.*

The dark blue F-150 Ford pickup truck entered the back parking lot, about two hours later. It pulled right up to the entrance at the Tires Center.

Once the passenger door opened and the interior dome light came on, Jack could see that it was Mrs. Terry, and she leaned over to the driver's seat and kissed the man. Jack wrote the truck's tag number on the inside cover of the Terrys' file.

He waited to see that Mrs. Terry walked through the Tires Center doors. Once verified, he followed the truck, staying back as far as he could, and did parallel street tailing also.

On one of the many turns made by the truck, he lost sight and thought all was lost, but then he saw it parked in the parking lot of an office building.

Jack was unfamiliar with the office building or any businesses on the street. He located a street sign that said, "Brandon Street." He drove by the truck and confirmed the tag number.

The parking lot was not full, but there seemed to be a lot of cars in it for 9:00 pm. He did not see a business sign or building number, so he decided to pull up to the front door to see what he could see.

Parking near the front entrance, he got out with a map in hand. As he walked toward the front door, he looked down at the map, with a straightforward plan. He was going to ask for directions to the local Sam's Club store. He hoped to find out if the man in the Ford truck was in the building.

As he got closer to the front door, he noticed security cameras on both sides of the door. But even more peculiar was that there were no door handles or knobs, not even a key port to lock and unlock the doors. There was a call box to one side of the doors.

What the hell? he thought to himself.

He was about halfway up the sidewalk, and he decided not to go any further. Jack's stomach started to churn, as he felt the hairs on his neck stand up. The sick feeling was his danger sign.

In what he thought was a natural motion, he stopped and looked around. Looking at the map and then looking off, as if he discovered what he had been looking for. He got back in his car and headed out of the parking lot.

He looked hard for an address or building number while leaving but could not find one. *The building to the right was 1223 Brandon Street, and the building to the left was 1227, so this building should have been 1225.* He noted as he left the parking lot.

The next day, as he reported to Daniel, he was so excited that he could hardly contain himself, and was talking too fast.

"Jack, calm down and take a breath. Take a moment to calm yourself, and tell me what has you all excited?" Daniel said, laughing at Jack and his excitement.

Taking a moment to breathe, Jack explained, "I used our membership at Sam's Club, and I was able to see the man that Mrs. Terry is having an affair with."

"That-a-boy good job! So, what's his name?"

"I don't have his name yet, but I did get his truck tag."

Jack laid out the events of the evening and asked, "Do you know anything about the buildings on Brandon Street?"

With some thought, Daniel said, "No, what's so special about them?"

Jack explained, "The building where I found the man's truck, on Brandon Street didn't have an address. Is there something special about that street?"

Daniel said, "I don't know much about the area, but I do know it is an area with Government Contractor's offices and off-base military offices. I don't know that building."

"Tell you what, give my buddy John Lasher a call. He and I go way back in the Navy, and he now works for the State Department, so he may be able to tell you about the building."

Jack called John Lasher later that day, providing him with the details of the building and asking for information. John promised to get back to him within a day or so.

"Say hello to Daniel for me, we had some good times in the Navy."

"I will, and thank you," Jack said, feeling good about the call.

After hanging up the phone, John noted in his call log that the call was related to the Brandon Street building and Daniel Draper. Every office had to maintain a phone log,

After three days, when Jack had not heard back from John Lasher, he tried again. Each time he called, he got his answering machine.

Jack did not leave any messages, *I guess Daniel is rubbing off on me. B*ecause Daniel was always preaching about not leaving messages on answering machines.

Jack told Daniel that John Lasher was not returning his phone calls.

"All I get is his answering machine. And no, before you even ask, I did not leave any messages."

Daniel surprised him, "John must be working on something crucial if he hasn't returned your calls. Only death would keep him from following up. Well forget about it, the case is dead anyway, we are off the case."

"What do you mean we are off the case?" Jack asked with a raised voice.

Daniel sighed, "I got a call late last night from Mr. Terry, he said that he wanted to drop the case. He said it was all a misunderstanding, but we are to keep what is left of the deposit for our trouble."

"What the hell?" Jack yelled. "Why is he closing the case? I found the man, and I know the kind of truck he drives, and I know where they meet."

"It is no longer our concern," Daniel said, "as a matter of fact, we were fired and will be paid for the work. After all, that is what we do, we work for the client and get paid for that work."

Jack was not happy, because he ferreted out the man, and was well on his way to finding out who he was. But Daniel was right, the case was over, so Jack stored the file in the secure storage building with other closed/completed files.

The next day, Daniel called Jack, "I have an out-of-town case in Texas, and I need a second man with me. Let me warn you, it has a little danger to it. You and I'll be out of town for about two weeks."

"What kind of case is it?" Jack asked.

"I'll tell you on the long drive. Make sure you pack clothes for long stakeouts."

Jack was ready to roll when Daniel came by at 5:30 am the following day to pick him up.

They filled the first couple hours on the road with small talk, and Daniel telling Jack about some stakeouts he had worked on. Jack always thought that Daniel was a badass, and after hearing about some of the old cases, he had a newfound level of awe for Daniel.

One of Jack's favorites was the case of the hoarse dog. Daniel began the story with a smile. "I was on a skip-tracing case with a partner named Tommy Battle, searching for Eric Newby.

There was a strange bounty on Newby, a Bail Bondsman hired us to find him, but not to apprehend."

"That is strange," Jack said, "What was the reason for not apprehending him?"

Daniel continued, "I don't know, but that was the assignment. We thought we found him held up at his ex-girlfriend's house."

"Ex-girlfriend?" Jack asked with a puzzled look on his face.

"Yes, ex-girlfriend, stop interrupting. For several days, we sat down the street from her house and could see the front and back doors. There was a five-foot chain-link fence around the house with vines weaved through it, the full length of the fence.

The drapes were always drawn, and the only person we could see going in and out was the ex-girlfriend. I had to get a look into the house, the only way was to get into the backyard and try to look through a window.

I decided to jump the fence while all the lights were still on, to see what I could see. Although we only saw the ex-girlfriend going in and out, at times we saw two shadows on the drapes.

The ex-girlfriend had a Doberman, which she usually brought the dog in around 8:00 pm every night."

Daniel paused, taking a deep breath before continuing his story. "So, one night, around 11:00 pm, I took off my shirt, and I had Tommy drive by the house slow enough for me to jump out of the passenger's side.

We had long removed the interior light bulb, so there was no light when the door opened."

Jack could see how the thrill and excitement of the night was coming back to Daniel as he told the story.

"Well, I jumped out of the car at about five miles per hour," Daniel continued, "I ran to the rear fence and paused on the outside, looking around and listening for any sounds.

Not seeing or hearing anything, I climbed up and jumped over the fence. I landed crouched to observe my surroundings and get my bearings."

Daniel took another deep breath and looked over at Jack. "And that's when I realized I had landed face-to-face with the girlfriend's Doberman. He looked at me as if to say, 'What fool is this?' I didn't move, we just stared at each other."

Jack couldn't hold back. "What did you do?"

"Well, my Seal training kicked in. Since the dog didn't bark, I knew it was a trained protector, not an alert dog. The advantage to me was that no one knew I was there. The disadvantage was that this dog was trained to attack when I moved.

My training, and his, were about to be put to the test. I knew he would go for my throat once I made any move, which was good."

"A good thing?"

"Yes, because that is when the dog would be the most vulnerable, with his neck extended the most. So, when I was ready, I stood up, and the dog launched for my throat.

I stood still until the very last moment, side-stepped to the left, wrapped my arm, at the elbow, around the dog's neck, and squeezed. I knew I had to hang on, otherwise, he would eat me alive. So, I squeezed until the dog stopped moving."

"You killed it?!"

"No, I just put it to sleep. The same sleeper move that works on humans can work on a dog if you can hang on long enough. I did get a peek in the rear window, and sure enough, Eric Newby was sitting on the sofa with his ex-girlfriend in his arms.

I jumped back over the fence and ran down the block to where Tommy was parked. When I jumped in, he yelled, 'What the hell?!' I looked like a mess, so I explained to him what happened, and we went to a local motel so I could clean up.

The Next morning, I called the Bail Bondsman and confirmed the location of Eric Newby. Before Tommy and I headed home, we drove by the house one more time to look.

As we drove by, the dog was outside, standing at the fence near the road. When the dog saw my face, he tried to bark, but his voice was hoarse, thus, the name, the hoarse dog story."

Finally, Daniel got around to telling Jack about the job they were headed to in Texas and why it was dangerous. "We are going to a little nowhere town in Texas, it has one primary industry, a rubber plant. The plant is unionized and there are reports of significant insurance fraud. The word is the union pays protection to the sheriff.

This plant has the highest per capita insurance claims in the South and the lowest employee turnover rate in the country. I have a list of twenty employees on disability, some temporary and some permanent.

We will spend the next two weeks observing and documenting these individuals. Still, we cannot contact or communicate with the sheriff's department."

After filling Jack in on the new case, Daniel was dog-tired and needed to sleep, so he asked Jack to drive.

"I need to be on my game when we get to the town. Since this is the first time you've been involved in such a case, your job is to follow my instructions, watch our six, and let me know if you see anything strange."

"Strange, like what?"

"You will know it when you see it."

On a long-deserted road in East Texas, at about 2 am, a quick jerk of the car awakened Daniel. He opened his eyes as Jack was correcting out of a slide.

"What happened? Did you fall asleep?!"

"No, there was a big tire in the middle of the road, and I almost hit it," Jack said, shaken by the experience.

"Well, hells-bells," Daniel said, "Let's go back and move it out of the road, the next guy or gal may not be as lucky."

Turning the car around, Jack headed back to the tire's location. But now, the tire seemed to have moved some.

Daniel said, "Slow down I can't quite make it out."

When the headlights hit what was supposed to be a tire, it moved. "What the hell?" Jack yelled,

"Stop the car!" Daniel yelled.

Starting to laugh, Daniel said, "That's no tire, it's a Diamondback Rattlesnake coiled on the road for heat in the night air. It is ten to twelve feet long! Stay here in the car and pop the trunk."

Jack heard him moving stuff back and forth and cursing the whole time. Finally, he came to the driver's window, and Jack lowered it. "Stay in the car, and if I get bit, run over the snake, pull me into the back seat, and haul ass to the next town about 45 miles away for help."

Jack looked at Daniel's face, then, he looked down to see what weapon Daniel was carrying to fight the snake. "A tape recorder?!" Jack yelled, "You're going to fight a twelve-foot diamondback rattlesnake with a tape recorder?!"

That is all Daniel had in his hand, a portable GE cassette tape recorder, the one with the pull-out handle on the front end, and the cassette door that popped open on the top. Jack could not believe what he saw next.

Daniel walked down the middle of the road, with Jack driving behind him. The bright headlights illuminated the scene, giving Daniel the appearance of casually strolling. Jack could not help thinking that as strange as this sight was, it was not out of character for Daniel.

As Jack watched, Daniel danced around the snake, and as it struck, Daniel whacked its head with the tape recorder. At first, it didn't seem to faze the snake, but after two or three more whacks to the head, it moved more slowly.

Daniel finished it off with a single downward slash of the tape recorder. Not only was the snake finished but the tape recorder was done for also.

Most people don't believe the snake story, however, the snakeskin is mounted and hanging in Daniel's living room.

When they reached the town where they were to do some investigating, they spent time driving around to get the lay of the land. The sun was starting to go down, so Daniel suggested they head for the hotel.

They pulled into the parking lot of the Lawson Hotel. Just as they stopped and parked the car, Daniel got a call on his cellular phone. It was his contact from the insurance company.

"Yes Bob," Daniel answered. "We arrived less than an hour ago. Yes, Jack is also with me. We have been driving around to get familiar with the place. We are at the hotel, getting ready to check in."

Bob told Daniel that the investigation had been canceled. "You guys can go ahead and check in for the night, we will pay for it. We will pay for your travel time and the hotel room."

"Bob, what happened? Why the cancellation after we got here?"

"There has been a new development elsewhere that changes our target." He wished them a safe trip home and a quiet night in the hotel. Jack had gotten out of the car and was at the back, waiting for Daniel to open the trunk. Daniel just stood by the driver's door with a puzzling look.

With a sigh, reflecting on how tired he was, Jack said, "What's wrong? Why are you just standing there?"

"The job has been canceled, and I have a very uneasy feeling."

"You're tired, let's get a room and crash for the night."

"Bob said for us to have a quiet night in the hotel."

Jack said, "That was nice of him, after all, they waited until we got here before they canceled the order."

"Yes, they did and will still pay our travel expenses and the hotel room, they'll also pay hourly for our time on the road. Now, that is a lot of money for no work." Daniels said to himself.

With frustration showing in his voice, Jack said with a very heavy sigh, "Well, what's the problem? Let's get a room, have a nice steak dinner on the company, and head home tomorrow."

Daniel said quietly, choosing his words carefully, "Insurance companies don't just spend money, especially if the error is theirs. Tell you what, get back in the car. We're heading back tonight."

Normally it was Jack who got the uneasy feeling, but this time it was Daniel. "Are you sure? We need to get some sleep."

Motioning for Jack to get back into the car, Daniel said, "We will drive for two hours and then get a hotel room. In the Seals, this feeling saved my ass on more than one occasion."

Daniel and Jack did not talk much while driving back out of town. They listened to music from the city's main radio station. As the radio signal was getting weaker, to the point Daniel was about to try and find a new station. Breaking news came through the static-filled speakers.

The radio DJ stated, "A fire has been reported at the Lawson Hotel. The fire department is fighting the blaze. Guests at the hotel have been evacuated. We'll keep you up to date as we learn more information."

Jack and Daniel just looked at each other. Jack said, "Thanks buddy, you may have just saved our lives."

Daniel said, "It never hurts to be cautious. Take Simple Work Insurance Company off our client list. We will not accept any more assignments from them."

During the journey back to Alabama, Jack attempted to engage Daniel in conversation about his SEAL experiences. All Daniel would say is, "We weren't there."

"What do you mean, you weren't there? You weren't where?"

Never taking his eyes off the road, Daniel said, "Exactly, we were never there."

"I don't understand, you were never...?" Jack shook his head and threw his hands in the air.

Daniel smiled and said, "It is this simple. If we were not supposed to be there, we were not there. If nothing interesting happened, that is where we were."

"Oh, I get it. It was all classified?"

"No because classified means we were there. So, since we were never anywhere interesting, there is nothing to talk about, and you will not ask again."

The rest of the trip back to Alabama was uneventful. Jack asked about Becky, "I don't think I ever heard what Becky did in the Air Force."

"Oh, she was in data entry." Daniel didn't offer any further details, or commentary on Becky's time in the Airforce. But there was something about the way he said it that made Jack think there was more to the story.

After getting back to Alabama, Daniel got another Texas assignment, one that would last two weeks. Jack had to handle several open cases by himself for the next couple of weeks.

As Daniel went over the open cases. *There it is again, that chill down my spine, and the hairs on my arm standing to attention.* Jack experienced that same feeling he had the night Daniel walked into his restaurant.

Trying to dismiss it, *Just nervous about being on my own with so many open cases. What can go wrong?*

CHAPTER EIGHT

Mary Rogers

(Protect the Terrys)

Mary confirmed with her superiors that she had been present when John contacted the PI, canceled the order, and closed the case.

There was one thing Mary and Denise didn't share with John, because it was at least two levels above his security clearance. Denise oversaw a specialized software algorithm designed to identify potential spies within the US Government.

She was the sole officer with knowledge of its workings. The program's original developer, who left the Air Force fifteen years ago, remained anonymous to all but Denise.

The program was known as A.P.C.S, (Advance Personnel Clearance Software). Mary Rogers was in the process of learning about the program and what it had uncovered thus far because higher-ups at the State Department weren't happy with only one person in the government being responsible for such a critical mission.

They had created a top-secret File of Discovery. An eyes-only file that was hand-delivered between department heads. "FD Communications," as it was called, is delivered in a securely sealed folder.

FD Communications allows each department head to familiarize themselves with the case subject and add their thoughts, ideas, and suggestions to the file.

Mary Rogers oversaw the project's transition and developed the protocols for training others. For the time being, Denise Terry reported directly to Mary Rogers, and Mary filed periodic reports with her State Department superiors.

A week after the meeting in John and Denise's home, Denise called Mary.

"I have not heard anything from Eugene. What should I do?"

"Go about your daily activities, and Eugene will make contact when he is ready to meet with you again."

It was late Thursday afternoon when Mary received an urgent call to report to her boss's office. Once she stepped into the office, he said, "Please close the door."

"Do you know Daniel Draper?" He asked, with a mysterious tone in his voice.

"Draper, Draper, Dra… yes, Draper is the name of the Private Investigator in my Denise Terry file. Why do you ask?"

"The Terry files?" he asked, "The file you just reported on earlier this week?"

Looking over his thin wire reading glasses. "What can you tell me about the Terrys?

Mary laid out the whole story again, as she thought to herself, *I spent hours on that debrief report, and he couldn't bother to read the damn thing.*

Mary explained how Denise Terry tried to work as an asset, and that Mr. Terry hired Mr. Draper to follow his wife, thinking Denise was having an affair.

Her boss started to shake his head. "So, this husband dropped a private investigator in the middle of your surveillance?"

Mary nodded, "Yes sir, a good one too."

Her boss rocked back in his chair, held his reading glasses in his right hand, and said, "Now this is starting to become as clear as mud. Your P.I. jumped in the middle of a hornet's nest, and no one knew it."

"I have a bad feeling, you are about to start swatting hornets. And you won't see them coming."

He continued, "See, Daniel Draper called a friend of his, John Lasher, who worked at the State Department."

"Worked?" Mary interrupted.

"Yes, worked, He was found dead at his home this morning."

Mary sat for a moment, then said, "What does his death have to do with Draper?"

Her boss said, "This is what we know. Lasher received a call from Draper. We know this because he made a note in his call log, and the topic of conversation raised a white flag with the NSA."

"The flag had to do with a building on Brandon Town Road in Huntsville, AL." Mary showed great concern as her boss continued with the story.

"The NSA's flag turned yellow+ when Lasher used his government cell phone to make a call to an unidentified party asking about the same building."

Mary said slowly, "And the flag turned red when Lasher was found dead."

"That's right," Her boss said with an intense look in his eyes, "I need you to get a hold of Draper and find out what is going on, he is now your responsibility. Oh yeah, prepare an extract and relocation order for the Terrys. Disguise it as a State Department TDY order for an undisclosed location; Just in case we need it.

Once I hear back from you, I'll be on the horn with both of their commands. We need to make sure they are safe."

"Yes Sir," Mary said as she got up to leave the office. She stopped and looked back at her boss, "Wait, who did Lasher call?"

With a steadfastness in his tone, he said, "We are working on that. And Mary, no more dead bodies on this file."

"I understand." With that, she was out the door.

Mary's first call was to Denise Terry. She explained that she and John might be in danger, and they needed to be relocated.

"Don't call John, I'll call him from my office, and do not go back to your home. The airport hotel shuttle will pick you up in the secure parking lot on the base. So, don't go to your car.

I'll make reservations for you and John at the hotel under the last name Stone, use your real first name. Margaret Washington, the hotel manager, will have special instructions not to require you to provide ID.

Mary initiated the process of relocating the Terrys to ensure their safety. She also secured authorization for temporary IDs and began arrangements for their permanent relocation.

She knew that the Terrys' disappearance had to be associated with their deaths, to protect them in the future. She reached out to a particular department in the FBI and assigned them to orchestrate a fictitious death event for the Terrys.

Mary now had time to reach out to Daniel Draper, she called him using the cell phone number John Terry had given her. She closed the door to her office, sat down at her desk, took a deep breath, and made the call.

"Hello," the male voice said on the other end.

"Yes, my name is Mary Rogers, and I'm looking for Daniel Draper."

"This is Daniel Draper, how may I help you?"

"Daniel, listen to me carefully, I'm with the State Department and need your assistance. To save time in getting you to understand that I'm legit and that I'm who I say I am, *I'll tell you things about you. Do you understand?"*

Daniel was familiar with the fast-track credential building and self-identification process as a Navy Seal. The sentence must start with, *"I'm going to tell you things about you."*

It was part of their security training and to be used when time was of the essence, and the speaker needed you to accept them as who they said they were – and receive the information they provided as gospel, without question.

Daniel gave the proper response, *"You don't know me."* If the speaker received any other answer, they could not continue. This signaled Mary that she could speak freely.

Per protocol, Mary told him his full name, date of birth, mother's maiden name, and name of his childhood pet, and she said, *"Pink polka dots, with green trim."*

The protocol required the speaker to add the color arrangement listed in the classified section of their personnel file, which the person put there for such an occasion.

"OK lady, you got my attention. What does the State Department want from me? I'm no longer in the Navy."

Mary outlined the events that had transpired regarding the Terrys and John Lasher. "Mr. Draper, you called John Lasher last week, asking about a building. I need to see your file regarding this building." She did not mention the Terrys or the fact that his friend was dead.

Daniel could have told Mary that Jack Campbell worked on the John Terry case and that he was the one who called John Lasher, but he thought better of it.

"Mary, I'm out of town," Daniel said," However, I'll be back home tomorrow, Friday Night, and can get the file for you out of storage over the weekend."

"Excellent, that will be great. Could you call me once you get home? So that I can note the time in my phone log." Daniel said he would, and they hung up.

Daniel started to call Jack to tell him about the conversation with Mary Rogers, but he got a sick feeling in his stomach. He got the same cramping in the field as a Navy Seal, just before ops went badly.

So, he decided not to tell Jack or his wife that the State Department had called about one of their cases.

Daniel was in Arkansas the next day, about five hours from home. He was looking forward to having dinner with the family for the first time in weeks. He called Becky and told her to expect him home for dinner and to let the boys know he had a surprise for them.

Mary Rogers was already on the State Department jet heading to North Dakota when her assistant, back in her office, received the call from Daniel. He said, "I'm just calling to let Mary know I'm pulling into my driveway now and will get the file out of storage, tomorrow for her."

The assistant was in the middle of asking Daniel to hold when she heard a bang, and the phone went dead. She tried to call back, but it just went to voice mail. The assistant called Mary on the jet and told her about the call and the bang.

Mary asked her staff to monitor emergency channels in the Huntsville, AL area. Within a minute, one staff member told her that one of Daniel's kids had called 911 and said his dad was shot in their driveway.

Mary started yelling out orders, "Have the pilot change course to Huntsville, AL. In this order, get the Alabama Governor, and then the Huntsville Mayor on the phone. Have the Special Agent in Charge for the local FBI office standing by waiting for my call."

"Oh yes, I want to talk to Dr. Fredericks at Huntsville Hospital!"

One of her staff reminded Mary that Daniel had a business partner, Jack Campbell. She gave orders to have the NSA monitor all phone calls in the Huntsville area and provided the trigger words for which to listen.

Her jet had already changed course and was headed for Huntsville International Airport when one of her assistants told her that Becky Draper had called Jack Campbell, and he was on his way to the hospital.

Mary had the governor give the State Troopers instructions to escort Jack to the hospital and ensure the route was clear of traffic. She had him call the mayor of Huntsville and confirm her authority.

And to block the city intersections to the hospital. She asked that uniformed officers bring any immediate family members to the hospital for protection.

Upon arrival at Huntsville International Airport, Mary immediately boarded the waiting Med Flight helicopter, which transported her directly to the hospital. Once in the hospital, Mary confirmed with the Hospital Administrator that the Chief Surgeon would oversee the Draper case.

She also reminded him that he was to report only to her. As Mary completed her instructions, one of her staff informed her that Jack Campbell had arrived at the hospital.

Before meeting Jack and Becky, Mary Rogers met with the FBI and the ABI. (Alabama Bureau of Investigations), the Chief of Police, and the Liaison for the Alabama State Troopers.

She provided only enough information to indicate the potential of a foreign threat and that The State Department was in charge. She also communicated with Base Command at Red Stone Arsenal.

Mary was under orders from her superiors at the State Department not to share any information with Jack or Becky. When she was ready, an Agent brought Jack and Becky into the room.

CHAPTER NINE
Eugene J Bullard

After his last meeting with Denise Terry, Eugene received a phone call the following day. He was told to report to Mark Quarles's office right away. Eugene figured that Mark, his on-the-ground handler, just wanted to get an update and congratulate him on an excellent mission so far.

Mark's office was in a building on Brandon Street. Eugene was at the building a week ago, he had to file his field report and confirm the cash amount given to Denise Terry. It's been a while since he had seen Mark.

When Eugene arrived at the Brandon Street building, there was a lot of activity. There were moving trucks, with men taking stuff out of the building. He stopped a man dressed in overhauls and asked, "What is going on?"

The man shrugged and said, "Guess you're moving."

As Eugene entered the building, the sounds of several shredding machines echoed from the rear end of the building, and people were packing up in the front offices. Eugene had seen this before, they were scrubbing the location.

Something must have gone wrong for them to scrub this site so quickly. He thought as he looked around for his handler.

After emptying a room, a team would sweep, mop, and spray a mist, creating a fog. Which was a unique formula that destroyed any natural material left behind. This included DNA and any finger, palm, and skin contact prints.

Eugene found Mark sitting at a card table, with two chairs, in the left front office of the building. Mark was his handler, and he only saw him when there was an issue or new assignment.

Eugene realized that no one ever called Mark by his last name. *I guess he is like Cher or Madonna, everyone knows who he is.*

He almost laughed out loud, but the thought he might be in some sort of trouble compelled him to hold it in.

He took a deep breath and walked into the office with Mark. The only thing on the card table was Mark's laptop computer. As Eugene walked in, Mark pointed to the only other chair in the room, "Eugene, please have a seat."

He wanted to ask what was going on, but he felt compelled to sit quietly until Mark spoke. After what seemed like an eternity, Mark finally looked up from his laptop and said, "Well, Eugene, how are you today?"

Feeling a little uneasy, not completely sure of what Mark was thinking, he said, "I'm good Sir, how about you?"

With a smile as fake as lipstick on a pig, Mark said, "I'm well also, thank you for asking."

Now that the pleasantries were out of the way, Eugene felt emboldened to ask what was happening. "Sir, what's going on? Are we moving?"

Mark looked at Eugene, without a smile this time, fake or otherwise. "Eugene, tell me about your current assignment and if everything is OK."

So, I was right, Eugene thought, *He wants to congratulate me on a fine job.*

"Yes Sir, all is going as planned. I saw Denise Terry a few nights ago and paid her more money. She doesn't know that she is being played like a cheap fiddle. In my next meeting, I'll reveal more of the true reason for my contact, and I'll pay her $30,000."

"By accepting that much, she and her husband will be in too far to back out and there will be too much for them to get command involved, that is not without going to jail themselves."

With that, Eugene leaned back a little in his chair, showing pride in his accomplishments.

In a quiet voice, but one that gave Eugene chills, Mark responded, "It sounds like everything is going to plan. Are there any complications, or have you noticed any special attention?"

"No Sir, for just a moment on the last night I was with Denise Terry, I thought I might have picked up a tail. But when I made some test turns, the car went on. So, it turned out to be nothing, but I'm glad I ran a test just to be sure."

With that, Mark turned his laptop around so Eugene could see the screen. On the screen was a video feed from the front of the building. Based on the time/date stamp, it was from the last night he was with Denise.

Eugene watched the screen and saw his truck enter the parking lot and park close to the building. He saw himself get out of the truck, head to the front door, and entered the building.

"Is that your truck in the parking lot? And is that you getting out of the truck and entering the building?"

Now Eugene felt a little fear rise inside, he didn't know what to make of the questions Mark was asking, "Yes Sir." He said with a nervous smile. "You can see that it's me, as I said."

In a voice that lacked emotions, Mark said, "Keep watching please."

In just a few minutes Eugene saw the car he thought was following him that night. The car pulled up near Eugene's truck, and a man got out of the car with a map in his hand. He started walking toward the front door but stopped about halfway.

He seemed to have had a change of mind, or something scared him. Getting back into his car, he did the strangest thing as he was leaving, he searched the buildings for something. He drove past the row of buildings, looking at the buildings on the left and the right, but drove off shortly after.

Leaning close to get a better look at the man, Eugene asked, "Do we know who he is?"

"Yes, we do indeed. He is a private investigator named Jack Campbell, who works for Daniel Draper, an ex-Navy Seal. Daniel Draper is married to Becky Draper, and her maiden name is Becky Anderson."

"Becky Anderson? Isn't she the one…?"

Mark interrupted in the middle of the question. "Yes, she is. Some coincidence, isn't it?"

"So that is why you are scrubbing this building, you think they are on to us?"

"Not sure, but we are not taking any chances, we are implementing all safety protocols. Just in case, we don't want you to meet with Denise Terry anymore. We will come at her from another direction. We want you packed and out of town tonight."

Handing a large envelope to Eugene, Mark said, "In this envelope is $5,000 and a new ID. We want you on the road. Leave all credit cards and current ID with me to shred, and head to Nashville, then make your way to the safe house in North Carolina."

Feeling a little more at ease, Eugene got up, took the envelope with the cash and ID, and gave Mark the old ID and credit cards in his wallet. Thinking to himself, *Damn, this could have gone a different way.*

Mark stood, they shook hands and Eugene left the building.

Mark Quarles was watching the Evening News when the News Anchor stated,

"I-65 North has been closed down due to a horrific single-car accident. The State Troopers said that the details are not clear at this time.

The most they could share was that a Ford truck with only one man in it was headed North toward Nashville when the vehicle flipped for no apparent reason. The truck burst into flames killing the driver.

The flames were so intense that firefighters struggled for several hours to put them out. The cause of the accident was unknown at the time of the reporting."

As the news report ended, Mark's cell phone rang.

"Yes, I saw it, good job. Call for the NC cleaner."

As Mark sat by himself, sipping on a glass of single malt scotch, he thought how relieved Eugene looked when he handed him the envelope. Holding his glass up, as if offering a toast, he thought, *Sorry Eugene, it's part of the job.*

Mark took a good long sip of his Scotch, reflecting on how decisions like the one he made that day didn't bother him as much as they once did.

CHAPTER TEN
The Terrys
(Only Five Minutes)

The call from Mary Rogers left Denise Terry shaken and very nervous. She could feel her hands shaking a little. She reached for the phone to call John but thought better of it.

Just as she was instructed by Mary, Denise went to the secure parking lot, and a cab picked her up. However, before she left the base, she asked the cab driver to pull over at the phone booth near the exit so she could call her husband.

The cab driver said, "Sorry, my instructions are to take you directly to the hotel and make no stops along the way."

"I understand the precautions that must be taken, however, there should be no danger in stopping at the payphone on base. This should be the most secure place I can be, and what are the chances the payphone on the base is bugged?"

As they approached the exit, the cab driver slowed down. He checked his rearview mirror, looked left and right, and scanned the area where the payphone stood. Not seeing anything that looked out of place, he pulled up to the payphone, and sensing no danger, he stopped the cab.

He parked, so the rear passenger door was right in front of the payphone. He turned to Mrs. Terry and said, "You have just two minutes to make your call."

OK, She got out of the cab with a smile and called John at his office. When he answered, she asked how long before he left for home. He said, "I got the call from Mary, and I was about ready to walk out the door. I was about to call for my cab when you phoned."

"I'm leaving the base now, I'll have the cab stop by your office and pick you up. That should save time and money."

Not seeing anything wrong with it, John said, "OK, your cab has to go by my office anyway. That would be great."

When Denise got back in the cab, she said to the driver, "My husband is ready to go, and he will be standing in the doorway of his office building. We must drive by there anyway. We need to stop and pick him up."

Since Mr. Terry's office building was on the same street they were taking to the hotel, and not a change in route, the Driver said he would stop and pick Mr. Terry up. Because there was no change in route, the cab driver did not have to radio his dispatcher to let her know of the difference in the fare route.

John and Denise Terry were glad to be together, but the call from Mary Rogers scared them. When John got into the cab, seeing his wife's lovely face reminded him that a couple of months ago he thought she was having an affair. He looked deep into her eyes and gave her a big kiss.

As it turned out, the cab also had to drive by the Terrys' street. Mrs. Terry convinced the driver to go by their home and allow them to throw some clothes in a bag.

The Driver resisted, "My orders are to take Mrs. Terry directly to the hotel. We have already made one divergence from my orders by going by stopping to pick up Mr. Terry."

John and Denise promised it wouldn't take more than five minutes, they would be in and out. The driver finally relented. He first drove by the house. The Terrys said, "It looks as quiet as it always does, nothing seems out of order."

Satisfied, the driver turned around at the end of the block. He pulled up to the curb in front of the Terry's house.

"OK, you only had five minutes. If you are not out by then, I will come in and get you. I will have to call Mary Rogers too."

John and Denise both got out of the cab on the right side. "It won't take us five minutes, we keep go-bags partially packed. We get calls to leave for temp assignments all the time." Denise said, as she grabbed John's hand, and they ran to the front door.

As they entered the house, John sensed something was off. John led the way as they walked into the kitchen and around the kitchen island. John saw the sliding door open, as he walked toward the door to close it, he heard a sound behind him.

He didn't see anything at first, but as he slowly walked back toward the hallway, he saw Denise lying on the floor, she was face up looking at him, but not seeing him.

"Denise!" He yelled as he ran over and kneeled beside her. He did not hear the suppressed sound of the handgun that shot him in the back of the head.

As the driver watched John and Denise enter the house, said to himself, *"I'll give them five minutes."*.

After exactly five minutes and thirty seconds, the driver got out of the cab and headed toward the house. As he walked toward the front door, he looked around to see if he could see anything that looked strange or signs of danger.

Once at the front door, he looked around one more time, and then he rang the doorbell. When there was no answer, he then knocked. When there was still no answer, he pressed his ear against the door. Not hearing anything, he turned the knob, and the door opened.

As the Driver stepped into the house, he called, "Mrs. Terry?" Not hearing anything, he started walking toward the kitchen, while calling, "John, Denise can you hear me?"

He first saw Denise lying on the floor as he entered the kitchen, face up, her eyes open, and a single bullet hole was in the center of her forehead. As he peeked further into the kitchen, just beyond the kitchen island, he saw John lying on top of her, with a single shot to the back of his head.

He heard some noise and looked quickly to his right, it was the sliding door at the back of the house. The door was open and a slight breeze moved the curtains just enough to make a slight scratching sound. Carefully and quietly, he backed out of the house, making sure he locked the front door behind him.

Once he was back in the cab, he radioed the dispatcher to call the police and Mary Rogers. He gave the address and said that the Terrys were dead. After that, he cut the radio off and threw his cell phone out the window. He also pulled over and pulled the tracking system out of his trunk, throwing it to the ground.

CHAPTER ELEVEN

HIDDEN KEY

(Mary Rogers and Pressure)

Daniel's shooting had taken a lot out of Becky. She and the boys, along with Jack, waited in the private hospital suite. While the boys were in the game area, playing a racing car game, she and Jack were sitting at the round table in the lounge area.

Using the disappearing ink pens she had in her purse, they had been writing messages back and forth to each other. In the last note Becky wrote to Jack, she mentioned the NSA and their protocols for surveillance.

As Jack was reading the note, Becky saw the panicked look on his face, and the way he started to write on the pad, she asked, "Jack, what did you do?!"

Just as Jack stopped writing on the pad, with the invisible ink pen, the door to the suite opened, and in walked Mary Rogers.

Jack tore off and balled up the top piece of paper, cupped it in his left hand, and touched Becky's leg under the table, she reached down and took the paper in her right hand.

Although Mary smiled, her eyes looked curious as she quickly scanned the room. The kids were asleep on the floor near the video game.

"I wanted to make sure you were OK. I have not heard any new updates, but since it has been a while since I spoke to you, I wanted to make sure you were holding up OK." Her words were friendly and showed signs of concern, as she walked slowly toward the table. "Do you need anything? Can I do anything to make you more comfortable?"

Seeing the notepad on the table and the pen in Jack's hand, not waiting for answers to the questions she already asked. "What are you writing? Is it a list I can help you with?" She asked as she started to reach for the notepad.

Jack realized that there would be indentations from his writing on the top piece of paper. He quickly scratched the pen back and forth all down the paper to show no ink was coming out. "I was going to make a list of things we need to do, but the pen is out of ink. We're also a bit too tired to make out any lists so it will have to wait for tomorrow."

Reaching for the pen Mary said, "Let me take that one and I'll get you a new one."

Jack quickly stuck the pen in his shirt pocket, "No worries, I'll keep it, and as I said, we can make a list later."

Mary picked up the notepad, seeing the indented lines down the page from Jack scratching the pen back and forth, she was satisfied that there was nothing written on the page. Jack could tell from her eyes that she knew he was up to something, but she didn't know what.

Mary looked at the pad once again, a new pad, with a page torn off. Just as she looked as if she were about to ask more questions, there was a knock on the door. The door opened, to reveal Dr. Fredericks, who came in with a big smile on his face.

Becky jumped up and ran toward him. His smile got even bigger as he grabbed her by her shoulders, looked into her eyes, and said, "He is out of surgery, not out of the woods yet, but he made it through surgery."

"That is wonderful news, when can I see him?" As tears of joy started to roll down her face.

Dr. Fredericks gave her a little squeeze and said, "One step at a time, we have him in a drug-induced coma and will keep him there for the next 48 hours and then re-evaluate. If all the signs are positive, we will stop the drug-induced coma, however, he might not wake up for 24 hours. The staff will bring him to this room in about 48 hours if all is going well."

Mary chimed in, "That is wonderful news, and we are all praying for his speedy recovery. Becky, do you mind if I go and speak with the Doctor?" Becky shook her head, and Mary said, "OK, you guys, go ahead and get some sleep. Doctor, let me talk to you in the hall." Mary and Doctor Fredericks stepped outside the door, and just before it closed, Jack and Becky heard Mary ask the Doctor when she would be able to speak to Daniel.

Once they were alone again, Jack said, "Confirmed," as he pointed to his right ear, indicating that he thought that Mary had been listening to them in the room. Becky just nodded her head as she sat back down at the table. She opened her right hand, unfolded the paper, and began to read what Jack wrote in silence.

"Daniel had me call a buddy from The State Department once to ask about an address I came across several months ago while working on a case. The guy never got back to me, and when I asked Daniel about it later, he just said, forget about it. So, I did."

She motioned for Jack to lean in close so she could whisper in his ear. "Do you still have a copy of the case file?"

Jack turned to her ear, "Only the summary file, the actual case file is in Protective Storage. The address would be in an archive file since it was not important to the case."

Becky knew what that meant, since Daniel left the Navy, he had always been concerned about keeping information files safe. He would say, "You never know what you need or why, but you do not just want anybody to have access to them."

Once the case was closed or stopped, all case files were stored in an off-site climate control security building called Protective Storage. Daniel did not trust banks because he knew how easy it was for law enforcement to get warrants to enter safe deposit boxes.

Protective Storage was an independent security vault company with an incredibly unique system to protect the customer's privacy. They offered safe deposit boxes, security drawers, free-standing lockers, and 10'x10' safe rooms.

Customers received a 16-digit I.D. card, using letters ranging from A through E. The letter indicated what type of storage container and in the middle of the I.D. number was the number of the security container.

The 16-digit I.D. issued to the customer was unique. It had no identifying customer information. The I.D. was logged in a ledger with alpha-numeric numbers for customer identification. The customer's identification was stored at another secure site, if someone came in with a key and did not know which storage unit or the 16-digit code and I.D. number, there was no way of identifying the storage container or the owner's name.

Jack whispered in Becky's ear, "I have to get out of here so I can see what I can find out."

She nodded and said out loud, "Well, it will be some time before we can see Daniel. I'll call my mom to come get the boys and take them to her house. That way, I can go home, clean up that kitchen, and get some rest. After a good nap and shower, I'll be ready for what is coming. I'll also bring a change of clothes."

Jack, taking Becky's clue, said, "That's a good idea, I need a nap and shower. I'll plan on returning here in, let's say, twelve hours or so." This conversation was for the benefit of whoever was listening.

Becky used the phone, dialing 9 for an outside line. Her mom answered, sounding as if she'd been woken up. "Mom, it's me. There is nothing wrong. Daniel is in recovery and the prognosis is good. I need some help with the boys."

"I'll be at the hospital in about 45 minutes."

Both Jack and Becky were napping when Mary entered the room to tell Becky that her mom was downstairs to pick up the boys. After taking a moment to orientate herself, she woke the boys, she led them to the door.

Talking to one of the men at the door, Mary said, "Becky is taking the boys down to her mother, and then Jack and Becky will go home for some sleep."

Mary spoke to Becky, "Your mom and the kids will have a protection detail. You and Jack will also have a man following you."

Becky took the boys to her mom in the waiting room, once there Becky held all three of them in a group hug.

"Boys, they do not know who shot your dad, but he is in recovery and is stable. The Doctor said we should know more in the next 24 to 48 hours. Since they are not sure of what is going on, to be safe, we will all have a protection detail."

"'One of these men," She pointed to the FBI-looking men, "will be following all of us, it is OK. They want to make sure we are all safe." After final hugs, kisses, and I love you's, the boys and their grandmother left the room.

Jack, and the man who was to follow him, waited until Becky and her detail had left the parking lot. Then Jack, and the man following him, headed for Jack's home.

Jack thought about how different it was driving on the crowded interstate in the morning, compared to the night before. He was never able to get his speed above 70 miles per hour.

The drive home gave him the most alone time he'd had since he went to the hospital the night before. This gave him time to think, and try and put things into some sort of perspective.

Ok, Mary didn't say so, but this all has something to do with The Terry case, and the reason John Lasher never called me back.

There was one bit of information in the stored file that might be helpful. *Maybe the tag number for the guy, Denise Terry was having the affair with, can be of help. I never did follow up to see who he was.*

Finally, he made it home, waved at his security shadow as he entered his house.

Once he opened his front door, he sensed someone had been there. Everything looked as if it was in place but to Jack, everything seemed off-centered just a little bit.

He looked at the dirty kitchen, and thought to himself, *I'll clean this mess up in the kitchen, take a shower, get a quick nap, and get away from that security tail.*

Walking past the dirty kitchen, into the bedroom, he plopped face-down on the bed, with clothes and shoes still on.

It was around 6:00 pm when Jack finally woke up, he looked at the clock on the nightstand and ran to look at the answering machine on the kitchen counter. There were no messages, meaning there was no update on Daniel. So, he decided to clean up.

Jack walked over to the window near the door, he peeked out to see if his protection was still there. Yes, there was a man in the black sedan, a Crown-Vic, the car most government people drive. Jack mused about the fact he referred to the Crown Victoria, cars popular with government officials and cab drivers, as a Crown Vic.

But it looked like a different man in the car, than one from the night before.

The thought occurred, *I guess there was a shift change in the last several hours.*

He turned and headed back to the kitchen, and that is when he saw it. The ink pen was on the table at the end of the sofa near the front door. This was confirmation that someone had been in his house. Things on that table were continually being knocked onto the floor as people headed for the front door.

There was a stack of unopened mail, a couple of magazines, and a pen on the table's corner. If someone knocked the stack to the floor, they would pick everything up and put it back on the table as best as possible.

Jack remembered, *When I got the call about Daniel, I knocked some items off the table. I picked everything up everything ... except for the pen.* Someone put the pen back on the table with the other items that fell to the floor.

Now Jack was sure someone had been in the house he needed to see if they had left any gifts behind. He kept an old portable A.M. radio, and Daniel taught him a trick with the radio. So, he got it and started to move slowly around, waving the radio back and forth.

He had turned on the radio and tuned it between stations so that all he could hear was static. Any radio signals in the room would disturb the radio static. The distortion would get worse the closer the radio got to the source of the radio signal.

He began in the kitchen near the phone and then in the living room around the sofa area. It did not take him long to find the first one, which was his clue to look closely for others.

He found a total of five bugs, one in the sofa area, one near the front door area, one near the telephone and answering machine at the kitchen counter, one on the nightstand in the bedroom, and even one in the bathroom.

Although he knew where they all were, Daniel always told him that if he found a bug, not to mess with it, be aware it was there, and it may come in handy to give off false information.

Jack picked up the phone to call Becky, figuring it had been bugged also. He called Becky at home and asked how she was doing, she said, "Right as rain." Jack understood that she knew the phone might be bugged.

He said, "Me too." Letting her know he knew they were being listened to. "Have you heard anything from the hospital?"

"Yes," she replied, "They called to let me know Daniel is resting, and they do not expect any change until the morning and suggest I get a good night's sleep and come in fresh tomorrow...." Becky paused as if in thought.

"What's wrong?" Jack asked.

"I just wish he was awake so I could tell him I love him."

Jack told her to get some rest, "I will be going back to the hospital tonight, and that way you can get some rest, and take over fresh in the morning."

Later that evening, when Jack was ready to head back to the hospital, he let the man assigned to follow him know where he was going. Daniel taught Jack to show every sign of compliance if he had an authorized tail and wanted to ditch it.

He would say, "You should do all you can to make them comfortable. By giving them the heads up and the destination of your trip and following the speed limit. When you get to your destination, wait on them before entering the building."

On the way back to the hospital, Jack noticed "Sam's Bar," two blocks up from the hospital. *I can be picked up there.* He thought as he drove by.

Once inside the hospital, he used the elevator to go to the fifth floor, he noticed that the bathroom and the stairwell exit doors were all in the same section of the hallway. With one plain-clothes guard in that section of the hallway and one in the waiting area, and as he looked down the hall, he saw another. The one down the hallway was at Daniel's door.

Jack saw a payphone near the elevators. He told the man with him that he would call Becky and let her know he was back at the hospital.

He went to the phone as if he was calling Becky, instead he called a cab company. He knew the number by heart, because he, would call them for customers when he worked at the restaurant.

"How long to get a cab to Sam's Bar?"

The Dispatcher said they were a little backed up, and that it would be about 45 minutes. Jack said, "OK, that is good, please send one to Sam's Bar. I'll be outside in 45 minutes with a blue windbreaker on."

Jack told his security that he did not want to wait in Daniel's suite by himself, so he sat in the waiting room. He found the opportune time to go to the bathroom and watched for a suitable time to sneak out the stairwell doors.

Just as Daniel always said, it was easier to sneak out of a place being guarded against intruders because the focus was not on who was leaving but on who was coming in. He smiled remembering this.

Jack was standing in the doorway of Sam's Bar when the cab pulled up. He ran and jumped in the car and ducked down in the back seat, "1389 University Drive please," he said as he raised his head to peek out the rear window to see if anyone was following.

The drive was less than ten minutes, and all he could think about was the file in the storage vault and what it could tell him about who shot Daniel.

As they pulled up to the front of the building, Jack noticed a black sedan down the street, it was just like the Crown Vic the agents were driving. He could not tell if anyone was in it.

"That will be $8.50," said the driver.

But Jack sat there trying to see if anyone was in the car down the street.

Finally, the driver said, "Hey buddy, if you want me to wait, I will, but pay me the $8.50 for the ride, and I'll reset the meter for wait time."

Jack said, "No, there is no need to wait. I'm getting out. But is there a place to get some coffee around here?"

"Yeah, Cathy's Diner about a block back on the same side of the street. Do you want me to take you back there?"

After Jack said yes, the cab driver drove around the block and stopped in front of Cathy's Diner. Jack paid the driver and turned to walk inside. The taxi drove back down the street, in the same way as the sedan, and as the headlights hit the passenger compartment, Jack saw two people in the front seat. Now he was a little scared, *Who the hell are they? Feds or the people who shot Daniel?*

Jack got a booth on the back wall of the diner, away from the windows facing the front doors. That was another lesson from Daniel. *The only thing you can be sure of is a solid wall at your back.* That was something Daniel always said.

The red-head middle-aged sever came to his table, Jack could tell she was a real natural beauty back in the day. Even though she had a very pleasant smile, her eyes told a sad story.

"What can I get you hon?"

"I'll have coffee and a ham and cheese omelet."

When she brought Jack his coffee, she said, "What's got you all twisted, hon?" Jack just looked at her, he was so focused on the car and what his next move would be that he completely missed her question.

"Sorry, what did you say?"

"Never mind," she said, "I can tell you're in another world. If you need anything, just let me know."

Jack sat there drinking his coffee and figuring out how to get into Protective Storage. In a short amount of time, the server brought Jack his omelet.

As she walked away, Jack noticed the register key hanging from her wrist, which made him think of the storage locker key on his key chain.

What am I going to do with the key? he thought. *Somehow the people in the car must have known about the secure storage locker and are watching the building, but who?*

No matter who it was, he knew he could not let them get a hold of the key. Jack took the key off his key chain and looked around for a place to put it.

As a former restaurant manager, he noticed the napkin dispenser on the table, which was the same brand he had worked with before. It would dispense napkins from two sides, with a cavity holding a spring to push them out. If you take all the napkins out of one side, the push plate can be accessed and tilted down, but how could he secure it?

He noticed the server was chewing gum and called her over.

"By any chance, do you have any more gum?"
She smiled, "Yes, sweetie, it's sugarless, is that OK?"

He smiled back at her and said, "Yes, you are a lifesaver."

He put the gum in his mouth, started chewing, and planned his next steps. He would secure the key, walk back down to the secure storage building, and walk in to see what happens next. Afterward, he would call for another cab to take him back to the hospital.

The flavor from the gum had disappeared. When no one was looking, Jack opened the napkin dispenser, removed the napkins from one side, and stuck the gum and key to the lower backside of the push plate. He replaced the napkins and put the dispenser back on the table.

Then he remembered that there was no way to know if this dispenser would be in the same place, or placed on another table, or how to find it.

Using his car keys, he carved an "x" on the bottom of the napkin dispenser, so he could find it without opening all the dispensers.

He got up from the table, left a couple of dollars for a tip, caught the server's eye, and motioned to the cash register, indicating he was ready to go.

After paying, and taking a deep breath, he stepped outside and looked up at the street, the dark sedan was still there. He walked to the secure storage building and entered the front door.

Once inside the door, he could see the office on the right side of the room with floor-to-ceiling glass as a front wall. *I don't know her.* He didn't recognize the woman in the office, so it was likely that she did not know he already had a storage container there.

He walked up to the open door of the office, and the woman behind the desk smiled a very welcoming smile.

"How may I help you today?"

Jack sat in the chair in front of the desk and pretended to be interested in renting a security box. She asked him questions about size and whether it would be for a temporary or indefinite period. She provided pamphlets of different sizes and their costs.

As they were discussing the options available to him, the front door of the building opened, and in walked Mary Rogers and two men. Jack figured they were the two men sitting in the car up the street.

"Jack," Mary started, "You gave us a scare, we looked for you all over the hospital. Good thing, one of our security details just happened to see you walking down the street and coming into the building. A secure storage facility? Why are you here?"

So, he was right, they were sitting on this building, but why? He had been in the building long enough that if he were opening a storage box, they would have caught him with it open and would have known the number.

"Why are you here?" She asked again as she looked at the woman behind the desk.

"He wanted information about getting one of our security boxes. We were discussing his options." The woman said. Jack sensed that she and Mary knew each other.

"Jack, I don't understand, your friend is in intensive care at the hospital, and you are sneaking out and looking for information on a storage box? Can you please explain?"

Jack paused for a moment, trying to find the correct emotional inflection as he explained. After giving a long low sigh, he said, "I felt useless and needed to do something. I have no idea what I could do to help with the case, but I thought coming here to research secure storage would take my mind off Daniel."

"So, you don't own a storage locker or box here?" Mary asked. He just shook his head no.

"Alrighty then," she said and motioned for the two men to stand Jack up. "My job requires I know things for a fact, I can't just take a person's word. Please take no offense, but I need you to empty all the contents of your pockets on the desk, and these men will pat you down."

After emptying his pockets, the men patted him down and found nothing, except a keyring with his house key, a car key, and what looked like an office key.

Mary said, "Sorry for having to put you through that, but right now, we have a man who has been shot, and we have no clues as to why. Let's get back to the hospital."

There was no conversation in the car on the way back to the hospital, but Jack's mind was busy. *What have I gotten ... no, what has Daniel gotten us all into?*

Daniel had repeatedly preached to Jack and Becky that you could trust the government to do the right thing, but this development wavered Jack's trust in Mary and whoever else was running the investigation. Now, Jack was 100% sure he had to get into the storage locker and see if he could figure out what was going on.

He had a plan, but he would need outside help. There was additional plain-clothes security when they walked into the hospital, and all exits appeared to have someone watching them.

Once inside, one of the men who escorted him back to the hospital said, "We don't want you and Mrs. Draper to feel like you are in prison. You are not prevented from moving throughout the hospital, however, you must let us know if you want to leave the building."

Jack nodded and said, "I understand, and I'm so sorry for any problems I caused by sneaking out."

"No problem," the man said, "OK, head up to Mr. Draper's room, 514 on the 5th floor. I'll let them know you are back and to expect you."

As Jack walked toward the elevators, he realized that he had no way of communicating with anyone outside. He knew they would be monitoring his and Becky's cell phones and any phone on the 5th floor. He had an idea, once in the elevator, he pushed floors 2, 3, and 4.

Jack decided to get off on floor two and see if he could find a way to call on an outside line. Once on the 2nd floor, he walked until he found an empty room. He entered and closed the door behind him.

Jack pulled a card from his wallet and called the number. A man answered on the other end.

"Woodruff here."

"Don't say my name, but listen to my voice, do you know who I am?"

Woodruff answered, "Yes I do, what's going on?"

"I have a double lap-full of crap and need your help."

CHAPTER TWELVE

CASH IN HELL CARD

(At What Cost?)

Officer Andy Woodruff was on the phone waiting for Jack to tell him what was happening. Again he asked, "What's going on?"

Jack let out a long sigh, and said, "I think I need to cash in the get-out-of-hell-free card. Are you still on the prisoner clean-up detail?"

"No," Woodruff stated, "I'm a Desk Sergeant on the 2nd shift. What have you gotten yourself into?"

"I don't have a clue, someone shot my boss, and there were State Troopers, and Feds..."

In the middle of the sentence, Woodruff interrupted him, "You guys were the ones who closed down the damn city and demanded a whole squad of officers at the hospital?"

"Yes," Jack replied, "But that is the thing, we got all of this attention and protection, but no one is telling us why."

"Who are we?"

" Me, my boss's wife and her family, have Federal bodyguards, and at the same time, they're trying to get information out of us and we don't know what to tell them."

"What in the world can I do?" Woodruff asked, "I'm just a local cop and have no pull with the Feds."

"Yes, but you may be able to get some information for me. I don't have the time to go into it now, give me a number at work so I can call you. It's probably best you don't tell anyone we talked."

Woodruff gave Jack the number to his direct line at the Shift-desk and told him to call him around 6:00 pm that evening. "If someone else picks up the phone, use the name James Baker."

With that, Woodruff hung up the phone. He stood still contemplating what type of hell Jack could be in. *With the Feds involved, this could be a career-ending move on my part.*

But Jack did him a solid with his ex-wife, and he did give Jack the get-out-of-hell-free card. *Hell, I owe him. I will do whatever I can to help, not sure how much help I can be.*

Jack hung up the phone from talking to Woodruff and ran up to the 5th floor of the hospital. Just as he came through the doors, the guards were standing by the elevator with curious looks. The stairwell door was only a few feet from the elevators. Jack told them he had gotten off on the wrong floor and ran up the stairs.

When Jack got to Daniel's room, Daniel was in bed sleeping, and Becky was fast asleep in a recliner near the window. This section of the suite with the hospital bed was like most other hospital rooms.

Jack tip-toed into the room and sat in a chair under the TV mounted on the wall at the end of Daniel's bed. Just as Jack was settling down, ready to catch a nap himself, the door to the room opened, it was Mary Rogers.

As she walked in, she asked Jack to wake Becky. Jack walked over and touched Becky on the left shoulder. She woke with an alarmed look on her face for an instant. Jack said quietly, "There's nothing wrong, Mary wants to talk to us."

Dr. Fredericks came through the door behind Mary, and they both stood by Daniel's bed. Looking at Jack and Becky, Mary said, "The doctors think it is time to reverse the medically induced coma and wake Daniel up."

Becky looked at Dr. Fredericks as if she received a lifeline of hope from him. "As I told Ms. Rogers, we are stopping the drugs that induce the coma, and we will bring him out very slowly."

"How long before he will wake up?" Becky asked.

Dr. Fredericks looked at Becky with a comforting smile and said, "We are going to ween him off the drugs very slowly, and every patient is different, however, we should know better in four to six hours."

As if she was too scared to hope, Becky asked. "Will he be…OK?"

With a slight smile, Dr. Fredericks responded, "We are very hopeful, the surgeon and his team did an excellent job. His chances are up from 50% to 75% or 80%. We will know more when he is awake."

As Becky was preparing to ask another question, Mary excused the Doctor and asked Jack and Becky to join her at the round table in the kitchenette area, away from the bed.

Mary started talking, and Becky and Jack could not believe what they heard. "John Lasher, an employee at the State Department, was killed after he received a call from Daniel asking about some unknown building on Brandon Street."

"Dead!" Jack said, with his mouth remaining open, "So that is why he never got back to me. But wait, why was Daniel shot? I made the call!"

This news caught Mary by surprise and for the first time, Jack and Becky saw real concern on her face. She said, "There was no information linking you to the call. Mary explained, "It has to do with how John Lasher noted the call in his call log. Instead of writing your name in the log, he wrote, "For Daniel Draper/building on Brandon Street."

After a short pause, Mary continued, "NSA reached out to State. My boss had me contact Daniel regarding the building on

Brandon Street since John Lasher did not put any building information in his log. Daniel informed me that he was out of town and would be home on Friday. Of course, you know what happened on Friday.

Daniel was to get the information about the case involving the Brandon Street building out of storage and was to let me know once he had it."

The situation regarding the storage place made more sense to Jack. *"So they were staking the place out."* Jack thought as Rogers continued.

"On Friday, he called my office to let me know he made it home and would get the case file over the weekend and call me on Monday."

Jack and Becky looked at each other. Jack's mind was working on the list of questions again in his mind. *Why didn't Daniel let you know that the case was mine? And why didn't Daniel tell me about the State Department's interest in the case?*

Jack concluded that Daniel was protecting him and Becky from whatever was coming. Looks like whatever he suspected was right.

Mary asked, "Do either of you know where Daniel has the file stored? How about you Jack? You must know about stored files from old cases." Jack used Daniel's technique to give an answer that skirted the truth but wasn't a lie.

"Daniel is the one who set up the office and files storage system, he said my job was to be in the field, not in the office." At that point, Jack said, "I would like to get something to eat and stretch my legs. Can I get anything for either of you?"

Becky was tearing up by this time, and Mary said she would stay with her. Jack started walking out of the room, looking back, his and Becky's eyes met. It was as if she knew he was up to something by instinct. Jack gave her a slight nod as he closed the door behind him.

Becky thought, *OK Jack, I hope you know what you are doing.* She allowed Mary to comfort her, hopefully giving Jack the time he needed.

After he left Daniel's room he turned left to head for the elevators. He started to take the stairs but decided to get on the elevator. Once on, while the doors were still open, Jack pushed the lobby button, where the cafeteria was located.

Once the doors closed, he then pushed 4, 3, and 1. When the doors opened on the 4th floor, he got off and pushed the button to go up. He used the new elevator to go to the 7th floor, two floors above Daniel's room.

Jack's head was spinning with so many questions, *Why didn't Daniel tell him that John Lasher was dead? Why didn't Daniel ask him to get the file out of storage and give it to Mary? Why did the simple question about the building on Brandon Street get a man killed and Daniel shot?"*

When Jack reached the 7th floor, he stuck his head out to see if there was anyone around. Not seeing anyone, he walked the hallway until he found a vacant room. Once in, he closed the door and put on the lamp by the bed.

The paper with Woodruff's work number was in his left shirt pocket. He pulled and called the number. When he got Woodruff on the phone, without giving him any information he said, "I have a file in Secure Storage. Do you know the building?"

"Yes I do, I used to patrol around that area. But don't I have to have some kind of special pass or key?"

Jack explained to Woodruff how and where he hid the key. "Now, once you retrieve the key, call me and let me know you have it. When you get the key, call my cell phone, let it ring a couple of times, and then hang up. Once I'm clear, I'll call you. Whatever you do, do not leave a message, or your name."

Jack stopped by the cafeteria, before heading back to Daniel's room, he picked up a couple of turkey sandwiches and bottles of green tea for him and Becky. He was hoping to have a moment alone with Becky so they could talk, but Mary was still in the room when he opened the door.

Around 11:30 pm Becky noticed Daniel moving and making sounds. Sticking her head out of the door, Mary asked one of the guards to get the doctor. Doctor Monroe, the surgeon, entered the room with two nurses.

This was the first time Jack and Becky saw the surgeon or any other doctor than Dr. Fredericks. Dr. Monroe asked Mary, Becky, and Jack to leave the room for just a moment.

While they were all in the hallway, Mary Rogers was off to herself. Her cool exterior was starting to show a little stress. She tried to link the information she had already, with the new stuff she learned in the last twenty-four hours.

What are the things that all of this have in common?

Brandon Street building

John Lasher

Daniel (maybe Jack)

John & Denise Terry

She felt that there was a missing piece, if only she knew where to look.

Although it was only about 10 minutes since the doctor asked everyone to step out of Daniel's room, it seemed like a long time before he opened the door and said that Becky and Jack could come in.

Mary insisted on joining them, but Doctor Monroe denied her access and said, "After the family has had a little private time, you can come in with your questions."

As Becky and Jack entered the room, the doctor held open the door. With a warm smile, looking directly into Becky's eyes, the doctor said, "I'll give you just a few minutes before I come back in, and at that time, I'll evaluate his condition, to see if he can answer questions from Ms. Rogers."

Becky and Jack both nodded to indicate they understood. After seeing Daniel in the bed motionless for the last day and a half, it brought them joy to see him with his eyes open and attempting to smile.

" Guys, I am so sorry for all of this commotion, and I thank both of you for being here. Are the boys here?"

"No sweetie," Becky said, crying again, "They are with my mom. They were up here all night."

Becky took a moment and offered a prayer of thanks to God for bringing Daniel through.

After words of comfort and relief, Jack told Daniel that Mary Rogers was out in the hall and was waiting to see him.

"Why didn't you tell me she needed a file from storage? I could have gotten it for you and given it to her." Before Daniel could respond, the door opened, and Mary Rogers entered the room.

At that point, Daniel strained to touch Jack's hand, and as Jack looked into his eyes, Daniel said, "Just like a tire in the road." Jack got the meaning right away. He was telling him not to trust Mary Rogers, she was not what she seemed. Jack knew that his and Becky's suspicions were correct, and Daniel had tried to protect them.

Mary asked Jack and Becky to wait in the hall, as she and one of the guards entered the room. The guard was carrying a mini tape recorder.

Mary had so many questions, she almost didn't know where to start. So she started with the question that seemed to have started it all.

"I am Mary Rogers, from the State Department. You and I have spoken over the phone about a national security issue. Do you remember calling my office?

Straining to be heard, "Yes I do."

"Was it related to the Brandon Street building?"

"Truth be told, I am not 100 percent sure, or how it relates."

"What can you tell me about the Brandon Street building?"

"It did not have a street address, that is why I had Jack call John Lasher."

"About that, he…"

Daniel interrupted her, "I learned of his death within hours of his body being found. I still have contact in many areas of the government."

"You didn't tell Jack or Becky?"

"Hell no! I called you. And guess what, I got shot."

Finally, Mary asked, "Where is the file on the Brandon Street building? And does it have anything to do with John and Denise Terry?" Mary was shooting in the dark with that question.

"Yes, that was the case we were working when we came upon the building."

A little snarky, Mary said, "You mean the case Jack was working when he came across the building?"

"Oh, you know that already?

Then Mary asked the question that tied everything together. "How did Jack come across the building?"

"He was following the military guy Denise Terry was having an affair with. The building didn't have a street address on the front, and it did not have door handles on the doors."

Mary abruptly said for the man with the recorder to cut it off. "For your safety, and the safety of your family, don't mention what you just heard here."

Jack noticed that Becky looked strange as they walked down the hallway to some chairs against a wall. He asked her, "What's wrong? The doctors seem to be happy with Daniel's progress."

For the first time since the shooting, Becky had time to clear her thoughts and think about the sequence of events. She knew the one place to get answers to a situation like this was from her former Air Force commanding officer, Denise Anderson.

Jack asked her again what was wrong. In an almost sad voice, she says, "I'm not sure. Something is not right, things are not fitting as they should. I need to talk to Denise."

"Who is Denise?" Jack asked with a puzzled look.

"She's someone I used to work with. If anyone can help solve this problem, she can"

CHAPTER THIRTEEN

Death In the Diner

Mary Rogers and the guard with the mini recorder were in Daniel's room for what seemed to be forever.

Finally, they came out, and Mary spoke to Jack and Becky. "We tried to find out as much information as possible, but he couldn't remember anything. He doesn't remember what the man in the driveway looked like or hearing anything suspicious other than the sound of the gun."

"He didn't remember being airlifted to the hospital; he said his only other memory after the shot is waking up this morning."

"See if you can get him to recall anything. The smallest of things could be very helpful in finding out who shot him."

With that, Mary turned and started toward the elevators. As she pushed the button to go down, she thought, *Damn it, I thought we would know something by now.*

After Mary left, Jack and Becky went back into the room with Daniel, he looked exhausted. Jack said, "I'll let the two of you have some time together; I have something I need to do."

Before Jack left the room, Daniel reached for his arm and pulled him close so he could speak quietly in his ear.

"The place is bugged; Mary might be with the NSA, not the State Department. Her job seems to control information. Get the Terry file from storage, and destroy it; do not give it to anyone." Jack nodded, said his goodbyes, and left the room.

As Jack left the room, his phone rang; he looked to see the number but did not recognize it. He let it ring then it stopped. He waited for the second ring, but instead, to his surprise, he got a "message" indicator. Jack clicked to hear the message.

"Hey, it's Woodruff, damn!"

Out of habit, Woodruff started to leave a message and remembered not to.

"Damn Woodruff," Jack said as he headed for the elevators. The hairs on his neck started to stand up, and he knew this could be real trouble if the NSA or anyone else was listening.

When Jack got onto the elevator, pushed the buttons for each of the three floors above Daniel's floor. He got off on the 6th but pushed all the floor buttons as he left. He found an empty room and called Woodruff just as he did before.

"Hello," Woodruff answered.

"Jack here, where are you?"

"I'm at the diner, sitting at the very back table."

"OK, I'll be there in about thirty minutes. Whatever you do, do not talk to anyone or make any more calls."

"I won't, and sorry for starting to leave you a message before; I was just so excited about getting the file for you."

"Stop talking! Do not say anything else; I'll see you in thirty."

After hanging up, Jack took the stairs down to the third floor and pushed the button for the elevator. When the doors opened, Mary Rogers and one of the plain-clothes guards were on the elevator.

"Where have you been?" Mary asked as they stepped off the elevator. "We thought you had left the hospital."

Jack said, "No, I have been just walking around on different floors. Now that Daniel is better, I needed to move around. You asked that I let you know if I left the building, so I just walked around on the floors to clear my head."

Jack caught the glance Mary gave the guard, and he got back on the elevator. Jack didn't know where the guard was going, but he had the feeling that he must get to Woodruff as soon as possible.

He said to Mary, "If it is ok with you, I'm going to get something to eat and sit for a little while. That will allow Becky to spend much-needed time with Daniel."

Mary said, "OK, but where will you go?"

"There is a diner just a couple of blocks; that way I'm near if needed."

"OK, just let us know if you go anywhere else."

Jack said he would and went to the parking garage and got his car. As he drove, to the diner, he checked his rearview mirror and parallel streets to see if he was being followed; he did not see any signs of a tail.

His heart was beating so fast after he parked the car and slowly approached the diner. Looking around, he didn't see anything strange. When he stepped into the diner, he immediately saw Woodruff sitting at the back table facing the door, but it looked like he was taking a nap.

Jack started to relax a little and smiled. He figured this cut into Woodruff's sleep time since he worked a night shift. He saw the folder on the table in front of Woodruff; Jack's smile got bigger as he was ready to make fun ... but as he got closer, something wasn't right.

The sounds from the diner's kitchen, which were loud as he walked in, seemed to fade away. The sights in the busy dining room, with customers, and servers moving around in organized chaos, typical for breakfast, started to dim around the edges of Jack's vision.

Jack developed tunnel vision, as he approached Woodruff slowly. The only thing he could see was Woodruff, and he did not hear or see anything else. Until he saw the Server go to the table to see if Woodruff needed more coffee.

She dropped the pot of coffee and screamed. Jack ran over for a closer look. Woodruff had been shot, a single bullet in the heart, and the file folder on the table was empty.

Jack backed away slowly and left the diner; his heart was racing. As he returned to his car, he looked around to see if anyone had followed him. He didn't know what to do; was he going to tell Mary about what happened or keep quiet?

He decided to drive by the building on Brandon Street, which started the whole thing, to see if he could see anything in the light of day that might help shed some light on whatever was going on.

It only took him ten minutes to get to Brandon Street; as he turned onto the street he thought, *Ok, Jack, take it all in, look for the stuff you can use.*

There stood the building, but it had an address across the front. "1225 Brandon Street," and even more shocking to Jack – the building was empty, with a **For Sale or Lease** sign out front.

When Jack returned to the hospital, he decided to update Mary, Daniel, and Becky simultaneously. He told one of the guards outside Daniel's room, "Please get Mary; I have something very important to tell her."

Once Mary entered the room, Jack retraced all his steps from the night Daniel was shot, including leaving the key in the diner down the street from the Secure Storage Company.

Seeing Mary's expression, Jack explained, "I decided not to share everything with you since I wasn't sure I could trust you. I am still not completely sure about you, but you're all we have."

Getting back to his story, "I called Woodruff from the hospital and asked him to get the key and meet me at the diner. Woodruff called to tell me that he had the file; he left his name in a voicemail, even though I told him not to leave a message or his name."

"Who is Woodruff?" Mary asked, hearing the name for the very first time.

Jack explained how he did Woodruff a favor on one of their domestic cases and that Woodruff was paying back the favor by getting the key and the file.

Jack laid out what transpired in the last few hours, with his voice shaking.

"I left the hospital to meet Woodruff at the diner; I was cautious about ensuring I was not followed, not even a parallel tail.

When I got to the restaurant, I saw Woodruff sitting at a back table; he looked like he was dozing off. Since he works the night shift, I just figured he was tired.

As I walked toward him, one of the Servers approached his table to freshen up his coffee. Once the Server got to the table, she dropped the coffee pot and screamed. I got closer, and I could see he had been shot once in the chest, and the folder on the table in front of him was empty.

I left the diner and drove by the building on Brandon Street, which started this whole thing, but now the building has an address, and it is empty with a for sale or lease sign out front."

Mary, Daniel, and Becky just sat and listened to the story. For the first time, Mary was starting to see the full picture, and that everyone was in more danger than she realized.

Mary was about to say something when the door opened. One of the plain-clothes guards motioned for her to step into the hall. She was gone for about five minutes, and when she returned, she was disturbed.

"Do you remember John and Denise Terry?" She asked, looking at Jack.

"Yes, I do; that was the case I was working on when I found the building on Brandon Street. Why what happened?"

She said with a sad expression and voice, "They were both shot dead at their home. Denise was working on an undercover case for the State Department. When you started tailing her, you inadvertently came across the subject of our investigation.

I had arranged to keep them safe in a hotel, but they decided there was no danger and wanted to stop at their home to pick up some clothes."

Daniel spoke for the first time, in a weak, but firm voice. "Now it makes sense; John Terry called me out of the blue and told me to drop the case and to keep any unspent expense money."

"Yes," Mary said, "I was there that night, he called per my orders. What we did not know at the time, was if the subject, Eugene Bullard, had spotted Jack. They also told me that Bullard was killed in a single-car accident. Bullard was the man Jack was following."

"Someone is doing a clean-up, taking care of all loose ends," Mary said almost as if she was talking to herself. "Once your guy Woodruff called your cell and gave his name, it was not hard for the operative at the NSA to track him down and have him killed."

"Oh, My God!" Becky yelled, "If they are cleaning up loose ends, what about Daniel and Jack? Aren't they loose ends? She said as she fought back tears.

Mary tried to reassure the three of them, pointing out that the only person who had contact with anyone was Jack, that he had met Mr. Terry and saw Eugene Bullard. She said, "The truth is, with the Terrys dead and Bullard dead, there is no longer any direct contact.

Based on what Jack told us tonight, the mystery building has been scrubbed. So, Daniel and Jack are not likely to be considered loose ends."

Praying she was right, and with no other signs of danger, the next day Mary reduced the security detail to just one person monitoring Daniel's floor and one in the entry lobby.

Daniel spent another two weeks in the hospital and was sent home with a physical therapy schedule. Mary had the State Department pick up all the bills and provide a Physical Therapist who was trained to watch for outside dangers.

Unbeknownst to Jack, Daniel, and Becky, Mary had put 24/7 non-intrusive surveillance on everyone. She told her boss that she was about 90% sure they weren't in danger. "But it's the 10% I get paid to worry about." She said as she left his office.

After a month, Mary started reducing the number of man-hours dedicated to making sure Daniel, Becky, and Jack were safe.

There were no indications of anybody looking after two months, so one Monday morning, Mary pulled all the remaining protection details, except for one man named Jerry Brown.

Late afternoon that Friday, Becky called Mary on an unsecure line.

Mary answered with an upbeat voice, "Well, hello there, how have you guys been?".

"All is well; Daniel is about 80% back to normal, Jack is doing a fine job running the agency, and I'm making it."

"So, how can I help you?" Mary asked.

Becky gave an unsure sigh, and said, "Daniel found some additional notes about the Brandon Street file. The notes are from when Jack sent Daniel his field report. No one remembered it until I started cleaning out an old box.

Not sure whether there is anything in it that means anything or not, just calling to see what you think."

Mary thought for a moment. "Well, it is probably nothing, but tell you what, I'm going to be in Huntsville on Monday; I'll come by your home and look at the information."

They said their goodbyes, and Mary noted the call in her journal and said she would go by the Draper's home on Monday.

But for tonight, I'm tired and can't wait to get home, open a new bottle of white wine, put on some soft music, and chill the rest of the night.

As she was pulling into her condo garage, her cell phone rang; it was Jerry Brown. "Hi Jerry, I know you want to know when you will be pulled…."

Jerry interrupted her mid-sentence, "Mary, the Draper's house was blown up! Jack and his date came by and surprised everyone by taking them out to dinner. They had just left when the house exploded."

With a bit of tremble in her voice, Mary told Jerry, "You are no longer on non-intrusive coverage; you are now on full-blown long gun protection detail. I'll have some backup for you within the hour. Stay with them; let them know you are there.

Take everyone to the airport hotel; I'll call you with the names on the reservations. I'm issuing Protocol Clean Slate, and they will have a new identity within 72 hours."

After hanging up with Jerry, Mary thought, *Jack has a girlfriend?*

She pushed a pre-programmed number on her cell phone, which called a secure switchboard operator.

The male voice said on the other end. "Operator, please state the reason for your call."

Mary said, "Code 34-zebra-alfa-David, today's color shoe size is a purple size 6."

"Yes State, how may we help you?"

Mary, using as much control as she could conjure up, "Case number 10566741-baker, protocol clean slate; I'll follow up in 72 hours."

"Your request has been noted; the call reference is Tango-24-Friday. Good luck."

Just as Mary ended her call, her phone rang again. She looked at the number and answered by saying, "You have Mary."

The male voice on the phone was Mary's boss, "Mary, I just heard from the NSA; the hit order was not for Daniel.

CHAPTER FOURTEEN

Hotel Room Surprise

Jerry Brown used his SUV to get everyone to the airport hotel, after talking to Mary Rogers and being put on full long-gun duty, including Jack's date, Marie Cates.

Every muscle in Jerry's gut tightened up, and his stomach began to churn, as he constantly searched for coming danger. He only had one clip in the gun and one full backup.

He knew that his muscle memory would kick in, short control bursts if shooting became necessary. He received his training, along with other special ops teams.

His concern was that there were so many moving parts with civilians. If things got a little hairy, he did not know how they would react at a crucial time.

He thought, *Well, Daniel would be more predictable, as an ex-Navy Seal. Maybe Becky could be counted on not to panic since she was ex-Airforce. But Jack and Marie, totally unknown.*

While everyone was waiting for additional backup, and Becky's mom and the boys, Jack talked about how he and Marie met. They had been dating for about three weeks.

"We met at Kroger's, she bumped my car with hers in the parking lot. After checking to see if she was ok, I could see that there was no real damage to either car. I said we should just let it go, and not even do a police report.

Marie, that is what she said her name was, insisted on paying me for the little damage that was on my car. I said I would take a coffee and Danish from the coffee shop across the way…"

Marie broke into the conversation, "Since he was cute, I said ok, and that I would buy him the best pastry in the shop."

The two of them laughed as if it was the best love story ever told. The kind of laugh that seems to come from young love. It was clear, that Jack had already fallen hard for Marie.

Jack picked up the conversation, "I liked her, so I asked her to go out on a proper date that Friday night. It was a simple first date, dinner in a nice atmosphere where we just talked."

"No worries. Glad to know you take your follow-up seriously."

"Yes, as a private eye, I must always be on top of my game."

"Ok, James Rockford, call me Wednesday."

Their first real date went very well. In fact, for the next three weeks, they had lunch or dinner together two to three times a week.

Daniel and Becky met Marie a week ago when Jack brought her to their house for dinner. Jack said, "That first dinner with the Drapers went so well; that is when I started to consider the thought that Marie could be the woman I had been looking for."

Tonight was to be the happy couple's first double date with the Drapers. But the Draper's home was bombed. Thank God Marie had suggested the double date with Daniel and Becky; getting them out of the house for the evening.

Everyone enjoyed hearing about the budding love affair, but Jerry found the situation a little disturbing, and he didn't know why. He thought, *There is something off here, Marie is not all that she seems.*

When Jerry and Jack were standing to one side, out of hearing of the others, Jack said, "If not for Marie's suggestion that we double date tonight, the Drapers' house would be a death scene investigation instead of arson." Jerry just nodded his head in agreement.

Jack looked over at Marie, *Odd*, he thought. *She was more rattled by the fender bender in the Kroger's parking lot than she seems to be by the bombing.* For the first time since he met her, he observed her more closely. *How can she be so calm?*

Jerry Brown had followed Mary's instructions by getting everyone to the hotel. Other Agents brought Becky's mom and the two boys to the hotel. Becky called her mom every five minutes, while they were on their way from Athens, to ensure they were okay and all were safe.

Since the agents Mary Rogers arranged had arrived from the local FBI office, Jerry felt he should separate the group.

As was his nature, and training, Jerry was constantly evaluating his surroundings, and options to ensure all under his control were kept safe. *With the kids and grandma in the same room, if there is a firefight, the chances of losing someone his very high.*

The more he thought about it, the more it made sense to divide the group. He had Becky's mom and the boys in one suite and Jack, Becky, Daniel, and Marie in another. *All of us can run and shoot if necessary. While Grandma and the boys are safe and out of harm's way.*

Becky protested; "I don't want to be separated from my mom and the boys!"

Jerry explained, "Mrs. Draper, I understand; however, it is for their protection. It is easier to keep them secure if they are not in the same room as you and the others. Also, you can talk to them on the phone all you want. The only thing is you cannot ask them their room number, and you cannot tell them what room you are in."

After protesting a little longer, Becky finally said, "Okay I understand. Just let me talk to them."

With that, Jerry picked up the phone that was on the counter, separating the kitchen from the rest of the suite. When the front desk answered, Jerry said, "This is Jerry Brown; please connect me to suite-baker."

After just a couple of seconds, Jerry handed the phone to Becky. "Ok, I have your mom and the boys on the phone."

Grabbing the phone, she cried as she talked to her mom and the boys. "I am so sorry for all of this, I promise you everything will be ok." After a few minutes of speaking to the boys and her mom, she was more at ease – so were the rest of the people in the suite.

Jerry left the room to call and follow up with Mary Rogers. Becky kept apologizing to Marie for spoiling her date night. "I promise you everything will be ok."

But something was bugging Daniel. He thought the questions Marie asked Jerry were too on point; more than the way a civilian would ask questions. Marie saw the way Daniel was looking at her. She was used to being around people like him and knew he was trying to work something out in his mind.

Walking over, and standing in front of Daniel, with a serious look, she said, "Montgomery-Montgomery-Montgomery."

Everyone in the room stopped talking, turned, and looked at Daniel.

"What did you say?" Daniel's eyebrows raised, as he cocked his head to one side slightly.

"Montgomery-Montgomery-Montgomery." Marie said again, this time with a look as if she expected him to respond in an approved manner.

Daniel was quiet for a moment, as he pondered the statement from Marie. Then he said, "South of Birmingham, and North of Mobile. Who the hell are you!?"

Marie replied, "Master Chief, we need to talk."

CHAPTER FIFTEEN
The White Paper

Pamela Smith did not know, nor had she ever met the Drapers, Jack, John Lasher, Eugene Bullard, Andy Woodruff, the Terrys, or Derrick Bass; yet her actions in the next eight hours of her work day would have a serious and profound impact on each of their lives.

While she wasn't surprised by the potential impact of her actions, she couldn't have predicted how significantly these names would affect her own life.

For the past five years, Pamela Smith had worked at the N.S.A. headquarters in Fort Meade, Maryland, serving as the Overseer of Document Control.

Because her position was misunderstood, some employees looked down on her. In fact, from time to time, she overheard people call her "The Paper Lady."

Pamela would only smile and think to herself, *Most people would be surprised to learn that my security clearance is just below that of the Deputy Director of the N.S.A.*

As the lowest junior agent in the command chain, she was referred to as Agent Pamela Smith when addressed verbally or in writing. The only people below her rank would be non-agents, such as the administrative staff, shredders, and cleanup crew.

However, her junior agent ranking was not reflected in her security clearance. Many of the papers Pamela delivered were low-classified items. However, because some documents might be High Security, Top Secret, or Very Sensitive, Pamela had to have the highest security clearance of anyone not in management.

She loved the Document Controller position because she was to interact with everyone in the building, depending on the documents she received. It was a very common thing to hear Pamela throughout the building asking staff about their lives.

Asking Sally about her kids, Robert about his dad's back, and even Bob about his dog. When she did hear someone looking down on her, she would think about her working hours and overtime pay for late-night work.

My hours are 8:30 am to 4:30 pm. My hours are 8:30 am to 4:30 pm. She would recite to herself over and over.

If she were required to work overtime, she would be paid "triple time" because overtime for her meant isolation.

Pamela was married to Bill Smith, who also worked at the N.S.A., but in another department. Because they had the same level of security clearance, they could discuss their work at home. That was a privilege other married couples within the agency with different security clearances didn't have.

Pamela passed up several promotion opportunities, she said, "I love what I do, and I love the freedom I have. The higher up the chain, the more freedom you lose." However, what she said was not the truth – Pamela Smith hid a secret.

Monday morning, Pamela arrived at work at her regular time, greeting everyone with a smile, and making sure she said hi to the downstairs receptionist.

"Good morning Sally, hope your Monday is going well so far."

"It is, but it is still early," Sally said with a smile.

Pamela gave a little chuckle, threw her hands up, and proceeded to the elevators.

Getting off on the third floor, she headed toward her office, which she referred to as the isolation chamber. Because it had no exterior windows on the outside wall, or glass on the interior walls, as the other offices did. This was an agency requirement because of the high-security documents received in her office.

She swiped her security key, hanging from the lariat on her neck, through the reader at her office door. As she entered, she could see the blinking light on the machine on top of the five-drawer filing cabinet behind her desk. Her heart seemed to always beat faster upon seeing the flashing light.

The flashing light was on the IBM Z299 machine, and it had only one purpose; to produce what is known as the White Paper.

When a historical event was linked to a currently active file or person, a report was produced called the White Paper. The information may include hundreds or thousands of pages and supporting documentation, however, the machine only produced a single page of white letter-size paper. On the paper is printed a series of numbers that refer to the case file and subsequent supporting documents.

Without cutting the lights on, Pamela walked over and pulled the white paper from the machine. "Let's go for a ride." She said out loud.

The ride she was referring to was from her office on the third floor, down to the Archive Agent in the basement, and then up to the Deputy Director on the eighteenth floor.

Without speaking, Pamela handed the White Paper to the Archive Agent. The agent logged the paper into the system, indicating Pamela as the presenter. After a long period of time, the Agent returned with several boxes in a cart.

Still with no words spoken, she handed a clipboard to Pamela to sign for the cart of information, and then Pamela was off to the freight elevator. Looking over her right shoulder as she walked away, "Barbara, tell your mom I said hello."

"I will, she asks about you from time to time."

With no other words spoken, Pamela pushed the cart onto the elevator, turned, and stood perfectly still as the doors closed, she saw Barbara turn away as the elevator doors came together.

Pamela wasn't to read any unsealed files, or tamper with sealed ones; although she didn't show it, she felt the pressure of time while Barbara stood watching her. She knew she did not have a lot of time. Unlike the passenger elevators, the freight elevator was faster.

As a trained speed-reader and gifted with a condition called hyperthymesia (or total recall, as it's often called) this meant that she could remember everything she saw.

Pamela swiftly scanned open file pages for reference numbers during the ascent from the basement to the eighteenth floor. There were no cameras on the freight elevators, so she moved as quickly as possible to scan any unsealed files.

She scanned as many pages as possible of the current case file and the names of the persons in the file. She only concentrated on the surnames and replaced the contents of the envelope. Making sure it was completely sealed.

When the elevator doors opened, Ruby Walker, the Deputy Director's assistant, was waiting for her. Per protocol, the Archive Agent called the DD's office to let him know the White Page files were on their way up.

Once she signed over the cart to Ruby, Pamela headed back to her office.

Back at her desk at 10:30 am, Pamela called down to the receptionist in the main lobby, "Sally, I'm ordering a sub sandwich for lunch from the sandwich food truck."

It was a requirement to inform the receptionist of outside orders. Once the order arrived, the receptionist would sign for the order and use an authorized card of the person to pay for the delivery.

All internal phone calls, both inbound and outbound numbers, were logged into a monitoring computer. The system would flag any number called for the first time, and suspicious numbers were flagged as well.

However, the conversations could not be listened to without a court order. Pamela called the sandwich truck, and when the woman answered, she said, "This is Pamela Smith in building 2313, I want to order lunch please."

The woman responded, "Hello Pamela, this is Jennifer, what would you like today?"

Pamela continued with her order, "I'm feeling a little nostalgic today, a simple meatball sub with red sauce on white bread. I was going to say let the cheese fly, but you better hold off, I'm watching my weight."

Jennifer said, "Excellent, we will have it to you within twenty minutes."

"That will be great, I just wish you could do it faster, but I know you will do your best to make it happen." The ladies said goodbye, and Pamela went back to her routine.

After hanging up the phone, Jennifer placed the slip with Pamela's order on the cook's wheel. She then pulled out what looked like a cell phone, but, it was a top-of-the-line satellite phone with a highly encrypted software package and an osculating signal scrambler.

Because of the osculating, no one could decode the signal even if someone could break the software encryption.

Jennifer pushed a preprogrammed button on the sat phone, and a male voice answered and said, "Please identify yourself and the purpose of your call."

"I'm sorry, I must have dialed the wrong number, please forgive me.

"No worries, where were you trying to call?"

"I thought I was calling tech support for my cell phone."

The male voice asked, "Are you secure?"

"Yes," said Jennifer."

The male voice said, "We recently changed our network and sometimes calls are misdirected. I'll transfer you to your needed extension."

There were a series of clicks and then a woman answered the phone. "Please identify yourself and the number and color of the day."

"Wanda Ice, 137 – orange."

"How may I help you, Wanda?"

Jennifer continued as Wanda Ice, "A field operative has been identified on the White Paper and his connection will unravel a host of others. This is just an initial alert, I'll have more information later."

"Thank you for your warning, please refer to item fox-trot, whisky-11 when you call in with updates." With that, the woman hung up.

Pamela called the main receptionist desk about ten minutes after placing her lunch order. Sally answered, "Yes Pamela, how may I help you?"

"Hey, Sally, when the delivery boy gets here with my order, call me so I can bring him a cash tip. I don't want to put the tip on my card this time.

"Of course," Sally said, "I'll let you know when I see him entering through the door, so he doesn't have to wait too long for you."

Pamela opened her middle desk drawer. Five single one-dollar bills were paper-clipped together in the left corner of the desk. She removed the stack of bills and the blank piece of paper was that was in the middle of the bills.

The paper was slightly smaller than the surrounding dollar bills and easily hidden in the middle of the stack.

Pamela wrote on the blank paper and placed it back in the middle of the one-dollar bills. She then folded the bills in half twice, so all that could be seen was a wad of bills.

At 11:00 am, Sally called Pamela to tell her that the delivery boy was coming through the front door.

"Thank you, I'll be right down. Please tell him to wait." Pamela said as she hung up the phone.

When Pamela approached the receptionist's desk, the delivery boy recognized her as a regular customer, and asked, "Why did you want me to wait? Did I do something wrong the last time?"

Sally and Pamela started laughing, and Pamela said, "No, not at all. I want to give you a cash tip because I didn't want to add it to my card. I'm sorry if you thought you were in trouble."

"Please give *Jennifer – your boss, a message for me*, tell her I'm very pleased with your service." The delivery boy smiled, as she handed him the folded bills. Without Sally noticing, Pamela gave the guy a slight nod. With a slight tilt of his head and direct eye contact, he indicated that he understood.

When the delivery boy returned to the food truck, he handed Jennifer the piece of paper that was in the middle of the dollar bills. The note read, "Not sure of context or order. The following surnames are related to the white paper: Terry, Anderson, Tyler, Lasher, Bullard, Draper, and Rogers."

After reading the note, Jennifer pulled out a sat-phone from her front pants pocket. She pushed a preprogrammed number on the keypad. The same male voice as before answered. Jennifer said, "Yes, this is regarding fox-trot, whisky-11." There were a series of clicks, and a female voice answered. "Please identify yourself and the reason for your call."

Jennifer said, "Wanda-ice fox-trot, whisky-11."

"What is the added information for this file?"

After Jennifer read what was on the note to the woman, she said, "That is all I have, no additional information at this time." The woman thanked her, hung up the phone, and Jennifer went back to her duties.

The N.S.A. listeners started to notice extreme chatter, however, no one could determine the subject matter or what was going on. News of the extreme amount of chatter made it to the Deputy Director's desk. What caught his attention was that the extreme chatter started within an hour of him receiving the White Paper.

William Robert Johnson was the Deputy Director of the N.S.A. and had been for the last ten years. He worked up the ranks, starting as a general listener of flagged phone calls. He made many jokes about his name (Billy Bob Johnson), and most people liked him at first contact. However, his first impression was misleading because it was part of his covert ability to blend in and not be seen as a threat.

For most of the afternoon, William had been pouring through the White Paper file material when something caught his attention and raised the hairs on his neck. The name John Lasher stood out because The State Department had generated an alert report regarding the death of John Lasher.

William used the name John Lasher as the focal point to filter other names in the file. John Lasher led William to Daniel Draper, Draper led him to Becky Tyler (Draper's wife's maiden name). Tyler led him to Denise (Anderson) Terry (Tyler's C.O. when she was in the Air Force).

The White Paper was generated because Denise Terry, Mary Rogers, Becky (Tyler) Draper's, and Bullard surnames were in a Federal Document Council. The F.D.C. is an eyes-only report shared between department heads.

William buzzed Ruby, his assistant, to come into the office. He asked her to retrieve the F.D.C-46-Sun file from the security cabinet. The security cabinet was a 5' by 5' walk-in cabinet vault where the top-secret materials were stored. Only William and Ruby had the scan card and combination to enter the cabinet.

Ruby retrieved the requested file and laid it on the small conference table in William's office, where he had the files mentioned in the White Paper spread out.

"There you go sir, do you need anything else?"

William was standing behind his desk, peering out of the window. Ruby could tell this White Paper was something huge, and there would be a lot of commotion in the next few days.

As if the question from Ruby had to travel some distance, he responded as he was heading to the small conference table.

"Please bring me any State Department transmissions related to the surnames Lasher, Rogers, Anderson, Terry, Tyler, Bullard, and Draper."

"Yes Sir," she said and left the office.

William sat down at the table and started to go through the F.D.C. file brought in by Ruby. The file consisted of five legal-size file folders and several computer disks.

As he laid the items on the table, stacking like things together, he said to himself, *Mary, what have you gotten yourself into?* Referring to Mary Rogers, the State Department person whose name was all over the files.

As William read through the files, he could see the connections but could not find the reason for the urgency of the

White Paper. At that time, Ruby came into his office with the State Department communications mentioning the surnames he gave her.

William reviewed the reports from Mary Rogers. The reports were regarding suspected spy Eugene J Bullard, with Denise (Anderson) Terry working as the field operative. He could also link John Terry to Daniel Draper, a private investigator married to Becky (Tyler) Draper.

He read that Daniel Draper was shot in his driveway, getting out of his car. William saw that Mary was assigned to the Draper's shooting because of his connection to John Lasher's death.

He felt very frustrated because he couldn't see it yet, but he felt that there was something right in front of him. He flipped back to the White Paper, hoping to find out why it was generated. He could see why the people listed and their connections would cause a general review alert. *But why the White Paper?* he asked himself.

Ruby knocked on the door gently, and then entered. She had additional State Department communications. The communications were addendums to earlier reports regarding Daniel Draper's shooting. After interviewing Draper, his wife, and Draper's business partner Jack Campbell, the supplements were added to Mary Roger's report.

William read through Mary's report, and nothing stood out, so he went back to the F.D.C. files and the earlier State Department communications, and that's when he saw it. He quickly flipped through Mary's report, now he knew why the White Paper was generated and why John Lasher was killed.

William pushed the blue button on his phone, which alerted the Department Heads of the top surveillance agencies to gather in William's office for an urgent "Eyes Only" meeting. He pushed the intercom button for Ruby,

"Yes Sir?"

"Ruby, get the State Department in here for an urgent eyes-only meeting,"

"Yes Sir."

William thought, *We need to add the State Department to the all-call button. They are potentially in the middle of the biggest espionage mess this country has ever seen.*

CHAPTER SIXTEEN

The Unknown Woman

William had NSA department heads to report to his office, including Maggie Walker, Bill Smith's boss, Bill is also Pamela Smith's husband.

As Pamela left her office for the day, around her usual time, her cell phone rang. It was Bill. She answered in her sweet quiet voice, "Hey honey, anything wrong?"

"No," He said, "But I'm a little behind and will be coming home just a little later, by maybe an hour."

Pamela released a sigh of disappointment and said, "Is everything okay?"

"Yes, just a busy day at work. We should have pizza and beer tonight, what do you think?"

Pamela smiled and said, "That sounds wonderful, tell you what, you order the pizza before you leave the office, and pick it up on your way home. I'll pick up the beer, how's that?"

Bill could tell by the tone in Pamela's voice that she was smiling. "That sounds like a plan," Bill said, "And I'll see you at home. Love you, see you after a bit." With that Bill ended the call.

Pamela knew that the White Paper was the reason for Bill being so busy, but she was not allowed to ask him about it. Their rule at home was not to ask about the other person's work assignments.

However, since they have the same security clearance level, they could discuss a topic if the other person brought it up. Tonight, she knew she had to wait for Bill to bring up the topic.

Bill was head of what everyone called the "Problem Solvers Squad," some of the most intelligent people the world had to offer. They enjoyed solving puzzles, finding hidden meanings, and decoding things that regular people couldn't interpret.

Pamela needed to know how far into solving the White Paper his team had gotten but she could not ask. *Glad he suggested pizza,* she thought, *that means more time for us to sit and talk.*

Bill and Pamela met in a speed-reading class, a little over four years ago. He was so shy, so Pamela made the initial contact and ensured Bill had an easy path to forming a relationship.

Back then, Bill felt so isolated in his personal life, because he could not discuss his work with anyone. It was as if fortune kissed him on the cheek when he discovered that Pamela, the woman from his speed reading class, not only worked at the NSA but also had the same security clearance as his.

He took it as a real sign, and after dating for a short period, he asked her to marry him.

It was the same type of planning, and laying of groundwork, that had been the key to Pamela discovering what Bill knew over the years. But, tonight, Pamela had to play it just right, to find out what Bill and his team learned about the White Paper.

As Bill entered with the pizza, Pamela handed him a bottle of beer and kissed him on the lips. After shedding his work clothes, he came into the kitchen in sweatpants and a white t-shirt.

Sitting at the island that divided the kitchen from the dining room, they talked about general family gossip but then, Bill stopped and stared at his beer bottle as if he were recalling something or he'd found a piece of a puzzle. Pamela was used to seeing that look when he had a breakthrough on a problem at work.

Pamela looked at Bill, reached across the island top, and put her hand on his. "Honey, what's wrong? You have that look you get when you're working on a tough problem."

Bill took a deep breath and said, "You got a White Paper today, right?"

"Yes, but I don't know what was in the referenced files."

"Yes, I know, it was eyes only. My team was called in to see if we could make some of the pieces fit. I just recalled something I first thought wasn't important, I just realized that it could be a key to the whole problem."

Bill told Pamela that his team was on the verge of busting an espionage ring in the government. With the glee of a child, he said, "The White Paper you delivered to your Deputy Director was the missing puzzle piece we needed. Along with increased underground chatter and a Sat-phone signal, all within an hour of you delivering the White Paper."

He took a swig of his beer, then explained, "For the first time, we have precise data, times, events of current news, and a Sat-phone signal that could be used to find this ring.

Up until now, we only had independent events that did not seem to be related. The Sat-phone is encrypted, and we have not cracked it. However, instead of cracking the Sat-phone, we can use the timing of its calls in conjunction with all other events to narrow our search."

Looking at Pamela with the excitement of a child getting a piece of candy, he said, "Just think, you may have delivered the piece that cracked this ring."

They spent another thirty minutes talking about the case and Bill was so excited he could hardly wait till morning. Bill kissed Pamela and headed in to shower before bed.

Pamela sat at the kitchen island, looking at the beer bottle her husband left behind. She had seen that look on his face before. Somehow looking at the beer bottle had given him a breakthrough. And she wanted to know what it was.

She moved to where he had been sitting, looking at the bottle, she thought, *OK, Billy boy, what did you see?*

Gazing at the bottle, she ran a list backward in her head. Pamela understood Bill's process when solving a problem and had gotten good at reverse engineering his thoughts.

She started the reverse list in her head,

- *Water droplets run down the bottle.*

- *The water droplets formed because of the cold beer inside and the warm air outside the bottle.*

- *He had taken several sips from the bottle.*

- *The bottle's twist top was already removed when he received it.*

- *Pamela had handed him the open bottle.*

- *Pamela bought the beer on the way home from work.*

- *Bill was late getting home from work because of an important assignment.*

- *The critical assignment was created because of the White Paper generated today.*

- *The White Paper was generated out of Pamela's office.*

- *Everything about today's assignment was because of the White Paper.*

Then Pamela saw it, she saw the pattern on the beer bottle. There had to be ten to twenty water beads on the beer bottle, and each flowed in its own direction. But they all had three things in common: The cold beer, the glass bottle, and the warm air surrounding the bottle.

To an average person, the water droplets on the beer bottle wouldn't have meant a thing. But to Bill and his team, the simple water pattern was more than just a sweating bottle of beer. Bill was like a bloodhound once he got on a trail. He would dogmatically run the trail to the very end.

Pamela guessed that the water droplets and their paths reminded Bill of the separate clues that the team had been following, trying to find a common relationship, which would lead to the covert agents.

Based on what Bill told Pamela earlier, today was the first time they could tie chatter to specific times and events of a sat-phone call. Bill knew the chatter started within two hours of the White Paper.

Pamela knew that Bill's team would comb through every bit of NSA data, calls, and emails to find another common link. Pamela thought *All you need are three points to find a common link.*

She knew that Bill or someone from his team would note that Pamela was the other thing common to the beer bottle and the White Paper. This would open a new line of investigation that had not been explored before. Pamela had to decide whether to wait to see if the trail would lead Bill's team to her or initiate "THE CALL."

After sitting and thinking for a little while, she decided to make "THE CALL." After all, if she waited until the team put it all together there would be no way out.

Bill yelled from the bedroom, "I'm getting in the shower now!"

"OK!" Pamela yelled back.

She got up from her seat at the kitchen island and opened the door to the pantry. She removed the step ladder from the back of the door and placed it to the left of the stove. Stepping on the top of the three-step ladder, she opened the top kitchen cabinet door, moved some glassware, pressed against the back of the cabinet wall, and slid the wall panel to the right.

This action revealed a secret compartment that held a Sat-phone, like the one used by the woman in the food truck. Pamela pressed a pre-programmed button on the Sat-phone and a male voice answered,

"Please provide your ID, Number, and Color of the day."

Pamela took a deep breath because she knew there was no going back once she completed the call. In a quiet voice, she said, "This is Papergirl, 1021, Green.

"Papergirl, is this a must-shatter the glass call?"

A must-shatter the glass call was when an agent was under deep cover, and someone's action may uncover them or at least make it impossible for them to stay covert.

"Yes."

"Please hold for Social Services."

This was Pamela's first time dealing with Social Services, a euphemism for the department in charge of Wet-work. Wet work consisted of cleaning up a location, or simply disappearing someone.

Social Services had to give permission, or at least be notified of any deaths or removals during an operation.

As Pamela waited for someone in Social Services to answer, she reflected on her life with Bill and the NSA. This was all about to change and she would miss it. She thought, *What a quirky kid you were when I targeted you in the speed reading class. I really ...*

A female voice came on the phone, "This is the Director of Social Services, please explain the service needed."

"Need permission to break glass regarding Bill Smith of the NSA."

"Is it your opinion that this is the best course of action, and you can defend at a later date?"

Pamela paused and gave a sigh, "Yes, if the glass is not broken it will damage the whole organization."

"Permission was given, authorization code victor-Xray-07-foxtrot. Good luck, Papergirl. Oh yes, remember you have to be in your handler's office to defend your action within 48 hours,"

"I understand."

With that, the phone line went dead, and Pamela put the sat-phone back in its secure location, ensuring everything was as it should be.

At 9:15 pm, 911 operator Janice received a call from a frantic female caller, the ID showed Smith. The phones and computers work together, Once the phone is answered, it automatically starts the audio recording.

"911, "What is the nature of your emergency?"

Pamela, trying to catch her breath, was crying uncontrollably. She was talking fast, and her words were running together.

"Ma'am, I'm here to help you, please take a deep breath and tell me what has happened."

Pamela took a deep breath and sniffed through the tears and her running nose.

"Yes, I need an ambulance for my husband. He has fallen in the shower and is barely breathing. Please send help right away!"

Janice read the address listed on the screen and asked Pamela to verify it was correct. Pamela verified the address and callback number. The questions served two purposes, one to verify identity, and the second to help calm the caller.

In as comforting a voice as she could, "My name is Janice, and I have First Responders on the way. In the meantime, are you near your husband?"

"Yes"

"Please look at his chest, tell me what you see."

"It is moving up and down, but just a little."

"Where is he located? Is he in the shower, on the bathroom floor, or in a tub with a shower?"

"He is in a free-standing shower, laying half in and half out on the bathroom floor. I didn't move him, but I laid a towel over his mid-section."

"OK, please move him to the flat surface of the bathroom floor if you can."

"He is too heavy, I can't move him."

"Ok, I just heard from the First Responders, they are one minute away. Please go to the front door and wait for them."

Pamela did as Janice said. Janice stayed on the phone with her until the First Responders came through the front door.

While the First Responders were working on Bill, a Police Officer came in to do the accident report. He was very considerate of Pamela's situation and only spent the amount of time needed to write down what happened.

Pamela explained how Bill went into the shower and about 10 minutes later, she heard a big thud. She said she called him, but he did not answer.

"I went into the bathroom, that is when I found him on the floor and called 911."

As the First Responders took Bill out, the police officer said, "Mrs. Smith, there are still some things I need to finish my report. You go ahead and ride in the ambulance with your husband and I will lock up once I am done.

"I appreciate you being so kind." She said as she climbed into the ambulance to ride with Bill to the hospital.

After the ambulance left, the police officer did a casual walk around the home. He did not see anything that caused him to question the Smith's marriage. He took a close look at the shower.

There was a smudge of blood on the wall of the shower, across from the shower head. The blood was nearly six feet high, he also noticed a bloody mark near the floor under the shower head. He completed his report, locked the front door, and left.

While Pamela was at the hospital, waiting to hear about Bill's condition, a detective came to speak to her.

"After reviewing the statement you gave to the Police Officer, reviewing the First Responders' report, and listing to the 911 recording, I've concluded that Bill's fall was an accident, and no further actions are needed."

"Thank you, detective, now all I need is for my Bill to wake up."

With that, the detective said his goodbyes and gave his best wishes for her husband's recovery.

As Pamela sat in the waiting room, waiting to hear from Bill's doctor, she struggled with the scene playing over and over in her mind.

Bill never heard her enter the bathroom, and the well-placed blow to the back of his head was as she had been trained to do. But the tough part was staging his body and placing some of his blood on her hands to place in the right spots in the shower.

The time she spent in the shower alone with him was the toughest, and she felt genuine remorse.

The following morning, Sally, the receptionist, called the Deputy Director.

"Sir, Pamela Smith will not be in today. She is at the hospital with her husband, Bill, he fell in the shower and hit his head.

"Wow, how is he?"

In a sad voice, "They are not hopeful he will make it."

According to the six o'clock news that evening,

"Thirty-five-year-old Bill Smith, a government employee, has died in the hospital from a severe head injury. Mr. Smith received a head injury after falling in his shower last night. A police spokesman said that it is more common than people think. According to the police report, his wife Pamela Smith called 911. Mrs. Smith was unreachable for comment."

The news commentators discussed that the news station had several calls because the neighbors were not used to seeing the police in their quiet neighborhood.

For the next two weeks, the NSA tried to find the solution to the sat phone puzzle. No matter how hard the N.S.A. team tried, without Bill Smith, the trail on the espionage ring ran cold after about a week and a half.

Before his fall in the shower, Bill sent Maggie Walker a text the night of the accident, saying he thought he found "The Key" and couldn't wait to show her the next day. Whatever The Key was, seemed to have died with Bill Smith.

The day after Bill's death, Pamela met with her handler, to defend her "break glass" actions. Three people were sitting behind a mid-size conference table. They started by asking her questions about her recruitment for the NSA, and her life at the NSA building.

After nearly two hours, the first member of the tribunal said, "Pamela, we will review all the historical data, and your decision to break the glass. Please report back here in two hours."

Pamela said she would and left the room. Since she had followed protocol, she was not concerned.

After Pamela had left, the tribunal discussed her actions and whether they were justified. One of the members said, "Yes her actions were justified, however, that is not the biggest concern at this time."

"What do you consider the biggest concern at this time?" Asked another member of the tribunal.

The third member said, "I think I know." As the other two members looked at her, she said, "We cannot look at Pamela's as an isolated incident. Yes, her actions seem to be justified and saved a lot of operatives. However, when we consider the network breakdown in other areas, it is clear we must do what we can to protect the network."

With everyone slowly nodding their heads, the first member of the tribunal said, "So, we agree the trail to this part of the operation must end with Pamela?" The other two members nodded in agreement, and the meeting was concluded.

When Pamela returned to the meeting place, only the woman member of the tribunal was present.

"It has been decided that you must be relocated to ensure that this part of the trail goes cold. We have prepared a letter of resignation to your boss and added some personal comments. Please sign it, and we will mail it today."

As Pamela signed the letter, she asked, "Do you know where I will be sent? I really enjoyed this assignment."

As Pamela handed the letter back to the woman, she said to Pamela, "All I know is that you will not be identified as part of this operation, and your trail will go cold."

As the woman was looking over the letter Pamela heard a noise behind her. Looking back, she saw three men dressed in all-white protective clothes. With a sense of alarm and an unanswered question on her face, she turned back to the woman in time to see her closing a door behind her.

As the great strength of two men grabbed her, and complete darkness covered her head, she thought, *I really did love this job.*

William Johnson was a little distracted by Bill's death. Although he did not know Bill well, William had worked with Pamela for several years and felt close to her. William recalled the item, which initially triggered the pushing of the "all-call button." It had to do with the reports from Mary Rogers and an activity review report generated by the NSA listening center.

The whole building was saddened by Bill's death, primarily because of their connection to Pamela. Everyone understood why Pamela wanted to take a couple of weeks off to deal with what happened, if not longer.

Three and a half weeks after Bill's death, Ruby was late getting into the office one day. William Johnson called her to see what was going on. "Hello William, I know I'm late, but the traffic has been blocked along the River Road."

"What happened?" William inquired, "Was it a wreck?"

In somewhat of a somber response, Ruby said, "No, it looks like they just pulled a body out of the river, and they have shut down the traffic so emergency vehicles can get to the location."

"Wow, do you know what happened?"

"No, I'm not close enough to see anything."

With a soft sigh, and care in his voice, William said, "Ok, be safe and I'll see you when you get in."

"Oh William, the mail would have been delivered by now, and placed on the right corner of my desk. Look through it to make sure there is nothing that needs your attention before I get to the office."

"Ok, will do, see you when you get here. Bye."

"Bye."

William checked through the mail on Ruby's desk, there was nothing that needed his attention. However, there was a letter from Pamela Smith. William took the letter back to his desk and used his letter opener to slice through the top.

The letter started with her expressing the joy and pleasure she had working for him at the N.S.A. But then the letter changed to a letter of resignation and a goodbye.

She wrote, "William, I hope you don't mind me taking the liberty of being so personal to call you by your first name. Although you are my boss, I feel close to you.

I find that Bill's death is hitting me harder than I thought possible, and because of that, I'll be moving back home to Georgia to be with my family. Please accept this letter as my two-week notice and waive the two weeks.

Please let everyone know that I'll miss them, and I hope we will have a chance to work together again. Take care William, and remember to take some time to enjoy life.

Sincerely Pamela Smith"

William took a moment to read the letter a second time. He felt for Pamela and what she must have been going through. He then said to himself, *The best thing I can do now is my job and help solve the problem Bill and his team were working on.*

As William turned his attention back to the White Paper issues, the question that kept nagging him was, *Why was Daniel Draper targeted?*

It was about forty-five minutes later that Ruby arrived at the office. She came into William's office, he inquired if she was ok, and made sure she did not see the body.

"I'm fine, and no, I didn't see the body. How about you, anything I need to hop on right away?"

William shared the letter from Pamela with her. Then he said, "We are going to do whatever it takes to solve the White Paper puzzle. Please see if there are any new State Department communication sheets with the surnames I gave you."

"I'll check the emails on my computer. If there is, I'll print it out and bring it to you immediately."

Once Ruby brought the updated report to him, he casually began reading it. Suddenly, William's face turned very pale. Lasher, Terry, and Bullard were all dead on the list, and Draper was recovering from his gunshot wounds. He yelled at the top of his voice for Ruby to come to the office.

Rushing in, "Sir, what's wrong?"

William said, "Get the F.B.I. and D.O.D. on the horn, I think we can prevent another murder."

Before Ruby left the room, she said, "I called a friend of mine who works at the police department. She said the body they found in the river was that of a woman, missing the head, hands, and feet. The body has been in the river for two to three weeks, to the best they can tell. The police are speculating that she was involved in drug trafficking."

William shook his head back and forth, "They keep finding people in the river missing parts of their bodies. That makes it impossible to identify who they are. Well, just glad it is no one we know, all our women are accounted for. Right?"

"Yes, all present and accounted for. I'll get the D.O.D. and F.B.I. on the phone for you," Ruby said as she left the office.

"Wait, never mind that. Just have Maggie Walker come to my office. Have her bring everything Bill Smith was working on and any notes from the White Paper project. I can't believe I didn't see this before."

CHAPTER SEVENTEEN
Marie Adams

Jack and Becky stood still, looking at each other in the hotel room; after Marie told Daniel that they must talk. Becky, with a confused look, and tone, "Daniel, What's going on? Do you two know each other?"

Jack, looking at Marie with an equally confused look, "Yeah, what is this all about? And what is this Montgomery, Birmingham mess?"

Daniel never removed his gaze from Marie. With a combination of surprise, intrigue, and awareness, Daniel said, with a quiet, authoritative voice, "Let me and Marie talk – and once I understand, I'll fill the two of you in."

Daniel and Marie stepped into the bedroom, standing very close to her he said, "OK, start talking, who are you, and what do you want?"

"Hold up Master Chief, I'm from Navy Intelligence. I was assigned to protect your group. My orders were to assess your safety and well-being, however, I couldn't identify myself unless it was necessary. "

Daniel relaxed a little, with the stress signs in his face fading some. He stepped back from Marie, as she continued.

"Command has ears in the NSA and your name kept popping up like popcorn. Your old Seal Team has been put on alert to drop everything and be on the next thing flying if I deem it necessary.

Now that Denise Terry is dead, Command feels it is even more critical to get you and Becky to safety. So, the Alfa team will handle your security once they get here.

I'll assist the State Department men who have been assigned until your Tier-1 operators arrive. Have you told Becky yet?"

Daniel cocked his head to one side, just as if a pet were asked if he wanted to go for a walk. "Tell her what?"

The Sat-phone Marie had in her shoulder bag rang at that moment, she retrieved it and flicked the communications switch, "Go for Adams. Yes, Sir, we need them – and Sir, make it fast."

After ending the call, Marie turned back to Daniel. "That was Command, Alfa team is on their way. It would have been much better if you had told Becky and Jack early on about your assignment."

Caught off guard, Daniel questioned, "Wait, you know about my assignment?"

"I was in the room, back in the shadow when command gave you your assignment," She said.

With regret and embarrassment in his voice, Daniel replied, "It might have been better if I told them, I just thought everything would be OK, and there would be no need to let them know."

Heading for the door and with purpose in her voice, Marie said, "Best to go out and clear the room, get Becky and Jack alone. I'll be the only one in the room when you tell them."

In a sheepish tone of voice, Daniel asked, "Could you leave us alone while I talk to them?"

With authority, she replied, "Master Chief, I have my orders."

Once back in the main room, Daniel said in a loud voice, "OK, I need everyone out but Becky and Jack."

None of the State Department Agents moved. Marie reached into her shoulder bag and pulled out her DOD badge.

She held it up for everyone to see and said, "You heard the Master Chief, we need the room." With that, all the agents left.

Jack and Becky stood looking at Daniel. Holding up his hand to stop any questions, he gestured toward the round table in the little kitchenette "I need the two of you to sit down, I have stuff to tell you."

Once seated, Becky asked, "Why is this woman calling you Master Chief? You have been out of the Navy for almost two years."

Daniel sat at the table, and Marie sat in a stuffed chair near the windows. Daniel said, "Well, that is a good place to start. I never left the Navy completely, I'm actually in the Navy Reserves, subject to active-duty recall and TDY assignments."

Jack couldn't hide the sense of betrayal in his voice, "You lied to me!"

Becky, sad and disappointed, said, "You lied to all of us!"

Shaking his head back and forth, and with a frown on his face, Jack almost whispered, "I knew there was a reason I could not shake the feeling that you were not telling me everything."

Almost in tears, Becky stated, "I would have bet my life that you would not lie to me."

Marie spoke up, "Tell them about your mission Master Chief."

"Stay out of this, you're a bigger liar than he is!" Jack was half standing as he yelled the words at Marie.

Trying to bring the heat down some, Daniel steadied his voice, "OK, you both have cause to be upset. Let me explain why I chose not to tell you everything. Marie, grab everybody a beer out of the mini-fridge, please."

Daniel waited until Marie had given everyone a beer. Then he started with his story. "First, let me say on the offset that it was not my intention to hide anything from the two of you.

However, if all had gone well, there would have been no need to share everything."

Becky asked, "Did the Navy ask you to leave, or was that part of your suitable cover story?"

Jack chimed in, "That night in the restaurant, that whole thing was an act, wasn't it? You had me feeling sorry for you. And how about the mishap with the C-4 during training? Did that happen? Something kept nagging at me, I felt you weren't telling me everything."

Daniel held his hand up again. "You both have all of the reasons in the world to be upset. Let me tell you everything and I think you will understand."

After taking a long swig of his beer, he started his story. "It all started one Friday night when I was told to report to Command immediately and not tell anyone. For us Seals, this is not so uncommon.

However, when I arrived at the headquarters, there were a lot of suits in the office. My C.O. did not bother to introduce the suits in the room to me, but a couple I guessed were CIA and there was one guy I knew from some work we did several months back, he was NSA.

I recognized one guy from the network news, he was a member of the Joint Chiefs."

Looking at Marie, he said, "I now know that there was another person in the shadow that I did not see. My Commanding Officer told me they had a credible threat to national security, and that my wife's life was in danger."

Becky and Jack looked at each other, and Becky started to ask a question, but Daniel held up his hand again.

"I promise to tell you everything. My C.O. read me in on the spy software you helped develop and put to work before leaving the Air Force. Your name appears in a very top-top-secret file. If your name is ever mentioned, all kinds of flags are raised.

Air Force Intelligence started to hear chatter about Denise Terry. When her association with you became apparent, a decision was made to put you under close non-intrusive surveillance.

However, they did not want to alarm you or alert any embedded spies that the government was searching for them."

With a thoughtful look, Becky said, "Wait, Denise Terry is the lady whose husband thought she was having an affair? The one who Mary Rogers told us is dead, along with her husband? But I never had any dealings with Denise Terry."

Daniel looked down at the table, then looked back up at Becky. "Denise Terry is Denise Anderson Terry, she was the C.O. of your department. Once it became clear that she was a target, Command decided to keep you under protective coverage.

It was agreed that it would be best if I went reserves, called to active duty undercover."

Daniel took another long swig of his beer and continued, "This is where it starts to get complicated, and I'll do my best to lay it out as smoothly as I can.

I was not privy to the source of the chatter, only told that the information came from a reliable source. I was told that there is a mole in the State Department and that we must be careful in sharing information.

Starting the private investigation firm was supposed to be a perfect cover. It would allow me to move around, investigate, and not look suspicious."

Becky, seeing the look on Daniel's face, said, "Something went wrong, didn't it?"

With a half-smile on his face, Daniel said, "Who would have thought Denise Terry's husband would call our firm to investigate his wife to see if she was having an affair?"

"Who would have thought he would contact us on the weekend I had to be out of town and Jack would have to take the case."

"Who would have thought I would ask Jack to call the State Department to check on an address for a building on Brandon Street?"

"Who would have thought I would get a call from Mary Rogers at the State Department while I was out of town, asking about that same street address?"

"That call from Mary made me suspicious, I knew something was wrong. I planned to put her off until I got home when I would bring the two of you up to speed, at least as much as Command would allow me to."

Daniel continued with a more serious look on his face. "Being shot in the driveway kicked all my plans out the door. It was not until tonight when Marie…." Daniel stopped and looked at Marie. "What's your rank?"

Marie said with military precision, "Lieutenant Marie Adams, Master Chief."

Daniel waved Marie over to join them at the table. As she sat down in the empty chair at the table, Daniel said, "Since I'm not up to date on what has occurred since I was shot, Lieutenant, can you update us?"

Marie took a swig of her beer. She said in a quiet calm voice, "I'll tell you what I can without providing sensitive information. I was called in by my C.O. and was told that I was being assigned to an undercover mission with National Security issues at stake."

"Like the Master Chief, I was not provided with the source of information. I was only told what was necessary to complete my mission."

"What is your mission?" Jack asked. "Was dating me part of your mission? Or did you add that in just for fun?"

Marie looked at Jack and said, "Hopefully, we will have time to talk about that, but I'm more concerned about keeping you alive for now."

Her response seemed to settle Jack down for the time being, as he recognized that his emotions were not the main concerns of the group.

Marie continued, "I know this so far, Denise Terry was the target. Foreign operatives were trying to get their hands on the software Becky helped develop. Mary Rogers, from the State Department, was Denise's handler."

"Denise had been approached by someone who promised a large cash payout. Their planned approach was to get Denise to clear some parts to be sold to an unfriendly nation. But that was a shell game. We are unsure how they would do it, but we know their target was the software."

Daniel spoke up, "But John Terry threw a big monkey wrench into the works. When he hired us to follow Denise, the plan of the foreign operatives started to unravel."

"That's right," Marie added. "The foreign operatives had no idea how much was known about their plans or who was involved. However, they started to panic and tried to cover their tracks."

"I understand that there was a lot of chatter caught by the NSA and other agencies. It became known that there was a mole in the State Department. But it was unsure if Becky had been identified, so I was assigned to help keep the three of you safe.

When your home was burned, I was told to reveal myself and take care of your security, and the State Department is being removed as your protector. I have requested the help of the Master Chief's Seal Team to take charge of your security. They should be here within in under two hours, they were already on alert, waiting for me to place the call."

Just as Marie started to say something else, they heard the electronic key open the hotel room door. It was Mary Rogers, with Agent Reed. As they entered the room, she had a very perplexed expression on her face.

Daniel, Becky, and Jack looked at each other. Jack tilted his head slightly as if to ask a silent question of Daniel and Becky. They both gave him a look as if to agree, *Yes, Mary Rogers must be the mole in the State Department.*

Mary and Agent Reed walked over to the table, and Mary asked in a demanding voice, "What the hell is going on here? Why are my State Department Agents standing in the hall? And who in the hell are you young lady, aren't you Jack's girlfriend?"

Marie reached into her shoulder bag, pulled out her DOD I.D., and handed it to Mary. "I have been ordered to take over the security for these three. Master Chief has been called back to active duty, his old Seal Team is on its way to help ensure their safety."

Mary argued with Marie, and all Marie would say was, "I have my orders, call your boss."

Finally, Mary pulled out her cell phone to call her boss. Mary was on the phone for about five minutes. After ending the call, Mary asked Mr. Reed to follow her out of the room.

Once Mary Rogers and Mr. Reed were out of the room, Jack turned to Marie, "Has it been confirmed that Mary Rogers is the mole at the State Department?"

Marie just shook her head from side to side. She did not directly answer, but Daniel understood that Mary Rogers was under suspicion.

CHAPTER EIGHTEEN

White Paper Missing Pieces

(She Was One of Our Own)

A very pale and trembling Ruby Walker entered the NSA's Deputy Director's office, without knocking, on Tuesday morning, at 9:45 am. William was sitting behind his desk, reading through reams of papers.

Upon hearing the door open, he looked up to see Ruby standing there. With a deep sense of concern, he asked, "Ruby, have you been crying – What's wrong – Are you OK?"

Without saying a word, Ruby stumbled over to the chair in front of William's desk and slowly lowered herself down. William hopped out of his chair and rushed around to her. "Hold on, let me get you some water."

He went into his private bathroom, and a few seconds later came out holding a paper cup of water. Kneeling beside Ruby, and handing her the cup, he continued to inquire as to what was wrong.

"Please tell me what's wrong. Do you need medical assistance?"

After taking a sip of water, and a deep breath, Ruby began to speak.

"I have some terrible news."

William didn't go back to his chair, he simply remained kneeling at Ruby's feet. He had never seen Ruby in such a state and didn't know what to do. Once again he asked, "What's wrong? Please tell me."

After taking another sip of water, Ruby asked, "Do you remember Congress passed a bill requiring government employees to provide blood samples?"

Thinking for a moment, William said, "Yes, the blood was collected and stored for a new DNA database. What has that to do with you?"

The corner of her lips turned up as tears started falling down her face. She tried to suppress the tears, without success.

She looked into William's eyes, with a very deep feeling of regret, and said, "As you know, our department completed the process three months ago. Today the first hit came back from the DNA data bank."

Trying hard to contain herself, she slurred the words out. "The woman they found in the river, without a head, hands, or feet, was Pamela Smith."

She then just started sobbing, letting the partial cup of water fall to the floor, as she dropped her face into her hands.

Perplexed and shocked, William tried to process the news he had just heard. He couldn't find the words, nor the emotions to deal with such tragic news.

After a couple of moments, he touched Ruby on the forearm and said,

"I am so sorry, I know you have known her longer than I have. If you need the rest of the day, just say the word."

"No sir, I think I will be ok. It is just such hard news, and the fact that I was stuck in traffic down the road, while they pulled her body out of the river, is so unreal."

After a little while longer, William rubbed her shoulder and whispered, "If you think you can continue the rest of the day, go into my bathroom and freshen up. Ruby, Pamela was one of our own, we need to solve this. I promise you, we will all take time to grieve once we find out what in the hell happened."

Fighting back more tears, she said, "I'll get myself together, and then I will be ready to assist however I can in solving her murder."

Ruby left the office, and William continued to sit on the floor for a couple of minutes more. He felt himself shaking a little, and he knew that if he lingered on the news of Pamela's death, he would be sobbing like Ruby.

"Pamela and Bill died within a month of each other. What the hell?" He said out loud. With that, he got up and went to the small conference table in his office. Stuff related to the White Paper was still laid out. After looking at the summary notes, he had prepared, Bill said aloud, "They killed our people."

After about fifteen minutes, there was a knock at his door, it was Ruby, "Sir, I'm better now and ready to do whatever you need me to do."

As William looked up from the table, he had a questioning look. After Ruby reassured him that she was OK and good to go, he asked Ruby to take notes.

He started by saying, "The first bit of business, I'll get with the Director, and we will draft an internal memo for all employees regarding Pamela. Once it is completed, I'll need you to ensure its distribution."

"Yes Sir, what can I do in the meantime?"

"I want you to do two things: get with Bill's former boss. I want a thirty-day look back on his activities through the time of his death. I want an hour-by-hour account of him on the day of his death."

After pausing, and giving the next request some internal deliberation, he said,

"Second, Please request an internal investigation of Pamela. Likewise, provide a thirty-day in-house review of all her activities. Since she was on leave when she died, get an hour-by-hour history for her last workday."

"You think they are related? Ruby asked, "I don't understand how. Bill died after a fall in the shower." Ruby said with bewilderment in her voice.

William sat with a thoughtful look on his face, and said, "I'm not sure how they are related, but my gut tells me that Bill and Pamela found something out and it got them killed.

Bill's fall in the shower could have been staged. So, we will collect the information on them, add it to what we know from the White Paper, and see if we can help solve their deaths."

William left the office to go to a meeting with the Director of the NSA, which lasted about an hour. The Director made the internal investigation regarding Pamela Smith official.

The Director said, "Yes William, that is a good idea. Everyone, including the receptionist, who had any contact with Pamela, will be required to submit a detailed report in writing…"

He paused in the middle of what he was saying.

"Wait, instead of reports, have everyone write up an internal 'memo'. The report would have to be filed with Congress, internal memos do not unless subpoenaed.

Keeping it as a memo means fewer people would see it. Thus, the spies embedded in our government have less of a chance of finding out what we know."

While William met with the Director, Ruby contacted Maggie Walker, Bill Smith's former boss. After exchanging condolences, Ruby passed on her boss's instructions to Maggie regarding Bill.

Maggie was apprehensive and said, "I don't understand the reasoning behind such a request. What is the purpose of such a report?"

Ruby could tell the request was not sitting well with Maggie, after all, she and Bill were close. His death hit her as if he was a member of her family.

To take some of the sting away, Ruby said, "It is William's thinking that Bill had found a key to the white-paper puzzle, and since he and Pamela had the same security clearance, he might have shared it with her.

If that is the case, they were both killed because of a clue Bill found."

After reconsidering the request, Maggie said, "OK, I will have the report compiled and sent over."

"Correction," Ruby said, "I have a text from William, instead of a report make it an Inter-office Memo."

Maggie rephrased and said, "I'll have the memo to you within 48 hours."

The mood was very somber back at the NSA, people found it hard to do their regular duties, but the added weight of the Pamela Smith memo was almost too much. The internal memo on Pamela was completed by mid-day the following day, Wednesday.

The memo on Bill was in William's office on Thursday by the end of the day. William did not look at it when he received it. He wanted to have fresh eyes once he got into the research. So, he put it in the box of White Paper files placed in the security vault until the following day, Friday.

Friday morning, William asked for Ruby to get a high-security temporary person to work at her desk for the day, so she would be free to assist with the findings. Once the temp person came to the office, Ruby took ten minutes to update him then she went into William's office to assist with the research.

Giving the memo from Bill's boss to Ruby, William instructed her, "I want you to go through this memo line by line.

Whenever you come across something that links to the surnames we have or any reported activities that seem odd, please make a note. We will compare notes at the end of the day."

William and Ruby worked through lunch. Ruby created a matrix to help cross-reference related items. There were many interesting points, but still, she and William could not get a handle on a precise pattern.

At around three o'clock, rubbing his right temple, William said, "Ruby, call Maggie, and ask her to join us. Also, have her bring her notes and any information Bill had passed on to her. I can feel it, we are looking right at it but can't see it. With her input, maybe we can make some headway."

Maggie showed up at William's office at four forty-five pm. William told Ruby to order coffee and sandwiches from the cafeteria because it would be a long night. The three of them, Maggie, Ruby, and William, spent an hour reviewing and talking about the things they knew. There was only one thing that Maggie had not put in the written reports.

"You know that he texted me that night?" Maggie said softly and with reverence in her voice. The way people do when remembering the last actions of a loved one who has died. Both Ruby and William paused what they were doing and looked at her.

William spoke first, "I don't recall seeing that in the reports, what did he say?"

"No, I forgot to add it to the report. I was not at my best for days after he died." Maggie said, with downcast eyes.

Ruby caught her eye, "We understand, we were dragging a little bit ourselves. What did the text say?"

Maggie smiled as if recalling precious moments. "It was not unusual for Bill to find a piece of a puzzle while he was relaxing at home, or even overnight while he slept. That is also why it didn't stick out. I was used to getting such a text in the middle of the night."

"What was in the text?" William asked.

"He just said he thought he had a breakthrough and couldn't wait to show me in the morning. That is all he texted. If he had texted anything more, security protocols would have kicked in on the cell phone. Of course, the morning never came."

Ruby and William looked at each other. Unbeknownst to them, after weeks of reviewing the data and spending several hours looking at the files, they recognized the same pattern Bill saw on his beer bottle.

"The cell phone!" William yelled, as he started pacing back and forth in the room, he said, "It is the sat-phone & chatter, they are the critical components of the whole thing. But not the way we were looking at them before."

Ruby nodded, slowly as if in agreement with William. Maggie sat and looked at both with a bit of bewilderment. She wanted to ask questions but decided to listen and observe. There had been a breakthrough, but she was unsure what it was.

William carried on, "OK everyone, push the stack of papers in front of you to one side. Flip your notepad onto a clean sheet of paper. Now, we will use the sat-phone calls as our pivot points and note the surrounding events, based on the memos we generated."

William suggested they start with the day Bill died and see what transpired. "Now that you have a clean piece of paper, about mid-way down the page, write 11:30 am."

"What happened at 11:30 am?" Maggie asked.

Ruby replied, "That was the first sat-phone call on the day Bill slipped in the shower. Using the prepared memos, we will chart what happened within our respective areas of responsibility."

The three of them spent the next three hours laying out the activities before and after each sat-phone call. They created a timing overlay for the increased dark world chatter of the sat-phone calls.

Everyone was surprised that one name seemed familiar to all targeted sat-phone calls. The three of them just sat looking at the papers before them. No one wanted to say it out loud, but it was clear that there was a clear line drawn to one person.

William said, "I don't understand, why is Pamela Smith's name all over this thing?"

Ruby suggested, "Since the White Paper was generated in her office, doesn't it make sense that her name would pop up as part of the background research?"

Maggie just sat there without saying a word. She was ready to point the finger at Pamela Smith for having more involvement than should be expected. However, she held her peace and let William and Ruby go back and forth. William tried his hardest to figure out a reason as to why Pamela seemed to have been near the start of multiple sat-phone calls.

Finally, William slammed his hand down on the conference table and said, "There is no way around it. Pamela was involved in some way."

Both Ruby and Maggie just nodded their heads up and down in agreement. At that point, Ruby said, "Well, we have another name that is all over these files. Mary Rogers is one name that just jumps out all along the way."

"Do we think Mary was working in some form with Pamela?" William asked.

With a contemplative look, Ruby said, "It would make sense."

Maggie then spoke, "This is the first time we have gotten so close to the heart of this espionage ring. I think it is time to start pulling people in, starting with Mary Rogers."

William was quiet for a moment, and then said, "OK, let's call it for the night, tomorrow is going to be busy. Ruby please, contact the Secretary of State, the FBI Director, and the Domestic Liaison for the CIA.

Tell them all to be in my office tomorrow, Saturday, at 9:00 am. Tell them we may have a breakthrough on an espionage ring.

Maggie, you and Ruby need to be here at 8:00 am so we can make sure everything makes as much sense in the light of day, as it does in the dark of night."

When the three of them left William's office, even though there seemed to be a breakthrough, a heavy spirit of gloom laid on them like a wet blanket.

For they knew that everything they thought they knew, about people they loved and trusted, would be challenged Saturday morning.

CHAPTER NINETEEN

All Yours Marie

(The Mary Rogers Exit)

After Mary Rogers left the hotel suite and was alone, her hands shook, and she felt as if her clothes were too tight. Everything had moved so quickly, she hadn't had time to process her own emotions.

She had been with the State Department for several years and was the handler for an untold number of assets. The bombing of the Drapers' house was the first time she came close to losing someone; it unnerved her more than she thought it would.

The elevator opened to the lobby of the hotel, and she sat down on one of the overstuffed sofas, trying to catch her breath.

The serene atmosphere of the hotel lobby clashed with the crazy chaos raging in her mind. All of a sudden she was hit with a case of the *what ifs. Suppose the Drapers were still at home?*

She couldn't stop shaking and was unsure if it was the bombing, or was it that she was upset with Marie Adams taking over. *OK, Mary, get yourself together.* She thought, *After all, somebody is trying to kill Becky Draper, and I have to stop them.*

She took a long deep breath and shook her head and shoulders, much as a dog might do to shed tension and stress. She patted her hair, and as she stood she brushed down her pantsuit.

After Mary got in her car, she called her boss again. "OK Sir, Marie has the protection detail, and I understand that Daniel's old Seal Team is coming in."

After Mary completed her situation report to her boss, he said, "Please pass on all secure information, and access codes to Adams."

"Mary, this is in no way a reflection on you and how you have handled things. It's just that DOD wanted their people overseeing everything. I hope you understand."

"Yes sir, I understand," Mary said, "I will go back in and give her the Protocol Clean Slate access."

"Wonderful, when you are done, head back to the office, the Secretary needs your assistance."

As she headed back into the hotel, Mary thought, *What could the Secretary of State want with me?* She put it out of her mind as she entered the hotel suite.

As she entered the room, Daniel, Jack, Becky, and Marie turned to look at her as she approached their table; not sure what to expect from her.

She smiled and said, "Lieutenant Adams, may I speak to you in the hall for a moment, please?"

"Sure. Excuse me, Master Chief." Daniel gave her a nod as she got up from the table. The two women went into the hallway and closed the door behind them.

Mary started, "Because of your high-security clearance, I'm about to give you something."

"I don't understand," Confused, Marie said, "I thought you brought me out here to yell at me some more."

Mary gave a fake smile and said, "No, not at all. We both have the same goal of protecting these people. And it is because of your assignment and security clearance I'm about to read you in on something.

You will need to memorize some critical information without writing it down. Are you good with that?"

"Yes," Marie said.

"I have issued a Protocol Clean Slate for this group. Since I have to step aside, I'm turning over the assignment to you."

"OK, what does that mean?" Marie asked.

With a solemn look on her face, Mary said, "When the Alfa Team gets here, you and the team will take the group to a specific secure location.

You are to tell the Team Leader to contact his command and tell them that the team is going dark under Protocol Clean Slate. Their Command will require them to check in every 48 hours, however, they are not to reveal their location."

"Yes, I understand," Marie said, "You can count on us to keep them safe. I must contact my command also. I must have permission to go dark."

Marie reached into her shoulder bag and pulled out the sat-phone. Mary walked down the hall a little piece, giving Marie space. After a little bit, Marie waved for Mary to come back.

Marie looked at Mary, with a combination of confusion and fear. "My command was already aware and said I should do as you say."

Mary asked, "OK, ready to copy the information?"

"Yes," Marie said, nodding her head.

Mary proceeded to give Marie the phone number she was to call; telling her it was for The one-time-only. "When the operator answers, say the following, acting for Code 34-zebra-alfa-David. Once you are recognized, say I'm calling for Tango-24-Friday.

The operator will give you the address of a secure location. There will already be a three-man team at the site. Their job is to ensure that the site remains safe, and once you arrive, they will make sure you guys are tucked in for the night."

Mary continued, "The new identification and background for everyone will be at the location. Any communications from the site will be made only by the military sat-phones."

"What about the kids?" Marie asked, "What will happen to them?"

"Oh, I forgot to mention. The boys, and their grandmother, are already on their way to the site. Anyone watching Jack, Daniel, and Becky is less likely to notice the move of the boys and their grandmother.

Tell Becky and Daniel that the kids have already been moved and that they are safe.

One more thing, tell Becky that "Becky" the software and a secured military laptop can be found in the safe at the safe house."

Marie looked confused as she asked, "What is Becky the software? And why is it named Becky, and what does that have to do with Becky Draper?"

Mary smiled slightly and said, "That is what this whole thing is all about. When Becky (Tyler) Draper was in the Air Force, she helped create a software program to aid in ferreting out spies in our military and governmental departments.

Her former commander was Denise Terry. Now that she is dead, Becky is the only one who fully understands the software. She is also the only one who can teach others to use it."

As she turned to walk away, Mary paused, turned back to Marie, and said, "Please tell them that I'm not a spy, nor the leak in the State Department."

With that, Mary turned and walked away. Without looking back she yelled, "Good luck, and keep our people safe."

Marie waited until Mary had gotten on the elevator and the doors closed before she headed back to the hotel suite. She paused at the door for a moment. All of a sudden she felt pressure all around her, and the heavy weight of responsibility to keep everyone safe.

She thought, Now *I have a national asset and her family's lives in my hands*. She took a deep breath and walked toward Jack, Becky, and Daniel.

They were still sitting at the round table. Although Marie tried to hide her anxiety, it was evident to everyone that something was concerning her.

Daniel was the first to speak, "What's wrong Lieutenant?" Marie was about halfway between the door and the table. She opened her mouth to say something when the Sat-phone in her shoulder bag rang.

She took the phone out and flipped the communication switch, "Go for Adams," she said as she stopped in the middle of the room. She stood there and listened to the caller.

"Yes Lt. Adams, this is Lt. Willmott of Bravo Team."

Marie said, "Copy that. How many in your squad?"

"We are a six-man squad," Willmott said.

Pleased with their strength, she said, "Excellent, leave two at the front entrance, leave one on the first floor at the elevator, and bring the other two up with you.

Once the three of you have reached our floor, leave one at the elevator to keep the door open, and you and the last man come to our suite – By the way, the Master Chief has been reactivated. Do you have a sidearm he can use?"

"Yes ma'am, I have orders to give him one."

Marie provided the suite number to Lt. Willmott and ended the call. Marie looked at the table where the three were sitting. She walked over and sat down at the table, and said,

"OK, the Tier-1 operators are here and will take charge of this operation. Three things before you pepper me with questions. 1st – You need to collect all your stuff, we are being moved to a safe house."

"2nd – Your mom and kids are safe, they are already at the safe house."

"3rd – I guess you heard me on the sat-phone, Master Chief, you have been reactivated and are now on active duty."

The Lieutenant coming up on the elevator has a sidearm for you. Mary wanted me to tell all of you that she is not a spy, nor is she the source of the leak in the State Department."

And with that, Marie excused herself and went into the bedroom. She called the number Mary had given her and recited the items she memorized.

After a moment, the female operator said, "Lieutenant Adams, we have been expecting your call. I'll provide the information to you, and you are to give the safe house location to the Seal Team once they arrive."

"Also, the new identities for your group are locked in the safe at the safe house. Your forefinger fingerprint is the only way to open the safe for the time being. We used your most recent updated fingerprints to program the safe."

"How did you know to program my fingerprint? I just learned that I would be protecting this group tonight."

Marie could tell the operator had a smile on her face when she said, "The safe is programmed remotely, that way, we can change access within moments of knowing a change is needed. Your entry will be deleted if something happens to you before you get to the safe house."

When Marie returned from the bedroom, she told Becky about the software, laptop, and safe. Becky nodded indicating she understood, while everyone collected their belongings, there was a knock at the suite door.

At the door, Marie yelled, "Lieutenant, I can help you with the bear." A predetermined code the Lieutenant and Marie had arranged.

The Lieutenant responded, "You'd better help the bear, I'm good." Marie opened the door and led the group into the hall, the Seal Team Lieutenant nodded and said, "Lieutenant, Master Chief, let's get your people to safety."

The trip to the safe house was uneventful with the Seal Team taking various precautions along the way. It was late when they finally arrived, and the boys and their grandmother were asleep.

Becky decided not to wake them, letting them rest, which she felt was the best thing for everyone.

The security team that was in place met with the Seal Team. It was decided that the security team would remain for the rest of the night, allowing the Seal Team to catch some much-needed rest.

The following morning was full of activities. Becky woke everyone up with the smell of bacon cooking. She cooked a nice breakfast of eggs, bacon, biscuits, and fried potatoes.

The boys, and her mother, were all excited to see that everyone was safe.

The Seal Team familiarized themselves with the property and its surroundings before taking over security. The security team that was in place stayed until after lunch. Finally, the Seal Team was in place for security, and everyone had settled down from the morning's excitement.

Jack found Marie outside on the front porch, he didn't notice that she was deep in thought, all he could see was that she was alone, and decided that was a good time to confront her.

"Can we talk now," He asked, but with a sharp tone in his voice, "Now that everyone is safe?"

Thank you, Lord, we made it safely... Her internal prayer was interrupted by Jack.

With a sigh, she said, "Yes, now is as good of a time as any. What do you want to say?"

Jack paused and took a deep breath, trying to control his emotions, otherwise, the discussion would not be very productive. After taking a moment, he said,

"Learning that we were just an assignment hurt. Because there were times when you could have backed off a little bit and kept your cover intact. Learning you were on assignment, made me feel as if I was just a diversion for you."

Marie stood there and listened to what Jack had to say. She made eye contact with him and did not try and dodge his gaze. After he seemed to have said what he wanted, she cleared her throat.

"I have thought about this a lot and wondered how it was going to end. I wondered if it had to end at all after my mission. Truth be told, it started as just a mission. That day in the Kroger's parking lot was designed so I could embed myself in with your group."

"However, as I got to know you, and the more time we spent together, I started thinking of you less as a mission and more as a wonderful man."

With a little smile on her face, "See it is all your fault. If you were not such a wonderful man, I would not have fallen for you."

Seeing that he was not amused, "But seriously, I do offer my heartfelt apology for not being able to tell you the truth, and the hurt it caused you."

"But know this, once all of this has settled down, and I'm no longer on this mission, I would love to see if there is any room to revisit our relationship."

Jack's response was not as enthusiastic regarding revisiting their relationship. However, at the end of the conversation, Jack was less mad. He said, "Let's agree to work together to keep everyone safe – and we will talk again after things have settled down."

Marie agreed and headed inside to get Becky started.

Becky was standing by the office door when she saw Marie, "I am ready to power up the laptop and get up to speed with the upgraded changes to the software."

"However, I'm not prepared to look at the current notes until I'm comfortable with the laptop."

Marie agreed and took Becky into the office. A lovely four-legged table was near the back wall. There was a window high on the wall behind the table, about half the size of a regular window, but spanning one-third of the wall.

As they entered the room, Marie said, "The table desk doesn't have drawers, however, the walk-in closet has two four-drawer metal filing cabinets and there is a four-foot-tall safe to store sensitive documents."

Marie retrieved the laptop and placed it on the table for Becky.

Before leaving, she instructed, "You'll find notepads and pencils in the closet. Remember to shred any notes or formulas before you leave. If it is something you will need later and don't want to shred, call me, and I'll put it in the safe."

Marie left the room, and Becky sat there thinking, *I left solitary rooms like this fifteen years ago, and here I am back again. But this time people are dying.*

CHAPTER TWENTY
Ask Becky

Ruby arrived early on Saturday to prepare for William's group meeting. She started a pot of coffee and retrieved a tray of pastries from the cafeteria, which was manned daily from 5:00 am to 6:00 pm.

Maggie and William arrived at 8:00 am and the three of them reviewed their notes from Friday night. They agreed Pamela Smith and Mary Rogers were involved in the espionage ring somehow.

At 9:00 am, the Secretary of State, the FBI Director, and the CIA Domestic Liaison arrived. The CIA cannot operate domestically, so a liaison department was established under the State Department.

Once everyone had helped themselves to coffee and a pastry, William spent the next two hours updating the group on the NSA's investigation into the espionage ring. He explained the process and the conclusions he, Ruby, and Maggie had reached.

The assembled panel agreed that Mary Rogers needed to be brought in for questioning. William asked the Secretary of State, "Do you know Mary's location?"

"Yes," she replied, "Mary is in my office updating files. Maggie called me last night and asked if I could have Mary nearby in case we needed to speak with her."

"Excellent!" William said, "By the end of today, we may have cracked an espionage ring we knew nothing about until just a few months ago. However, I'm torn between being proud of our progress or being embarrassed that this ring was operating under our noses."

William instructed the FBI Director to send Agents to the State Department to pick up Mary Rogers for questioning. "Just tell her she is needed to assist with an inquiry on which she may have information."

"Have her here at 2:00 pm. Let's the rest of us take a lunch break and be back here by 1:30 pm."

When the group reassembled in William's office, they talked about what they had for lunch and how this meeting messed up their Saturday plans with their families. Ruby noticed their nervousness before the confrontation with Mary Rogers.

When the two agents approached Mary in the State Department office, at first she didn't think anything about it; after all, it was not completely unusual for such requests. But on the ride over to William's office, she sensed that this was not a typical request.

There was no small talk in the car, the agents sat quietly and just stared out the front window. A knot started to form in her stomach, and it seemed to grow tighter the closer they got to William's office.

Mary Rogers walked into William's office at 2:05 pm, with the two FBI Agents behind her. Seeing the assembled group, Mary felt the knot in her stomach get tighter.

William spoke, as the others remained quiet, "Ms. Rogers, please sit in the empty chair in front of my desk." The others had been arranged in a semi-circle around William's desk.

William asked, "Mary do you know why you were asked to come to this meeting?"

Mary looked at everyone present, including her boss.

"No sir, I'm not quite sure why I'm here. However, I suspect it has something to do with the case I have been working on for several months."

William nodded "Yes, that is correct. There is an espionage ring within various branches of our government and military branches. We have not been able to find them or stop them from operating."

"For the first time, we have uncovered information that could lead to the shutting down of these spies. Last night we learned that one of our trusted employees in the NSA was somehow involved with this group. Also, we determined that there is a leak in the State Department."

With that, William stopped talking and just looked at Mary. Everyone was looking at her as if they expected her to yell out, *"Yes, it's me."*

After a few seconds of silence, Maggie cleared her throat. "This group has reviewed the information gathered by the NSA, and we all agreed to bring you in for a conversation."

"We are not stating that you are the leak, however, a mound of evidence points in your direction. This is your opportunity to settle the question."

Mary's eyebrows furrowed as she leaned forward, her tone firm but controlled. Not showing any emotions, Mary said, "I would like to see what possible evidence you could have that I'm involved with any spy ring or have leaked any non-public information. Please show me what you are talking about."

Although Mary tried to project a level of confidence, and signs of outrage, the knot in her stomach had tightened to the point that she had to force herself to breathe.

"OK then," William said as he laid out the information and all the trails that led to Mary. He showed her everything, except the sat-phone junctions, and the Pamela Smith connection.

At the end of an hour and a half, William sat quietly in his chair, as the rest of the group was deathly quiet. He looked at Mary and said, "As you can see, all trails seem to lead back to you as the leak."

Mary sat quietly, then said, "This is the closest we have ever been. First, I'm not the leak, but I can see how you came to that conclusion. Second, what did **Becky** produce? This is the most collected information, and **Becky** should have great results."

Everyone just looked at each other with questioning expressions on their faces. Finally, Maggie said, "Who is Becky, and what does she have to do with this?"

With a look of surprise, and somewhat shocked, Mary said, "With all this information and the connections, you have made, I thought you got it from **Becky**. "

William yelled, "Who is Becky!"

After taking a deep breath, Mary said, "**Becky** is the code name given to the software Denise Terry used to detect foreign intruders, or spies, within our government and military ranks."

"She gave it the code-name **Becky**, named after Becky Tyler. Becky Tyler is now Becky Draper. The software was given that code name because she was the one who developed it."

William asked the Secretary of State if she knew about the software, to which she replied affirmatively. "We were under orders not to share the information with anyone or any other agencies because we discovered that spies may be embedded in every agency."

"As we now know, you had one in your own agency. Pamela Smith was a trusted employee and now we know she was a spy."

With anger and embarrassment in his voice, William snapped at the Secretary of State, "Get this Becky Draper in here now!"

The Secretary of State said, "We can't. Mary Rogers had issued Protocol Clean Slate for her and her family, and we don't know where she is."

William sat back in his chair, sighed loudly, and groaned. Ruby asked, "What is Protocol Clean Slate?"

The FBI Director said, "Protocol Clean Slate is a complete wiping of the subject's ID, with the issuance of new ID, and relocation. There are no public records of the new ID or the new location."

"However, since Mary issued the PCS, she is the only person who knows the new names and new locations."

Everyone looked at Mary, once again with the expectation of her providing the needed answers.

Mary said, "Sorry, I don't know the new information. I wasn't the one who received the new information when it was issued."

"Well, who in the hell has this information?" William demanded.

Mary said, "I was removed away from the investigation, and ordered to pass the authority to receive the information to Lieutenant Marie Adams of Naval Intelligence."

"Adams, and the former Seal Team of Daniel Draper, have taken Becky, Daniel, and Jack to a secure location."

"They are all off-grid, and the only way to contact them is through the Navy Seals Command. The Team is to check in with their command every 48 hours."

Looking at William, Mary said, "I suggest the NSA prepare an eyes-only pouch with all your collected information. Contact Navy Seal Command and direct them to get the pouch to Lieutenant Adams for Becky Draper

William looked at Ruby and said, "Make it so, and let me know how fast they can get the information to Becky Draper He turned to the Secretary of State and said, "I highly recommend that you restrict Mary's access to unsecured information until we get to the bottom of this."

The Secretary of State nodded and asked Mary to turn over her security badge. She did so and asked, "May I go home?" William said it was OK and the Secretary of State nodded.

After Mary left the room, the group spent the next forty-five minutes debating whether it was a good idea to let Mary roam free while they waited on the results from **Becky**. William asked the FBI Director to put a blanket on Mary.

Ruby asked about the 'blanket,' and the FBI Director explained it would cover all digital communications and include constant surveillance.

William asked the Secretary of State to inform the group as soon as he had any information on **Becky**. With that, William dismissed everyone and asked Ruby to put everything in the secure safe.

Before William and Ruby left the office, Ruby noticed a worried look on William's face. "Sir, what's wrong? Why do you look so worried?

"I think we just green-lit a hit on Becky Draper."

"I don't understand, what do you mean?"

"If there is an operative working close to any of the department heads that were here today, it won't be long before they know the importance of Becky Draper, and they will take her out."

CHAPTER TWENTY-ONE

Team Becky

Becky Draper spent the next several days in the office at the safe house. After eating breakfast with everyone, and spending a little time with the boys, she would lock herself in the office. Someone would bring her lunch.

Around 7 pm, she would come out for dinner, chat with her mom, and play with the boys. After the boys had gone to bed, she would go back into the office and work until around 2 am.

It was very demanding, and the pressure of knowing that Denise Terry was killed, just added to her sense of urgency.

"I refuse to look at the new information until I am up to speed on the upgraded software." was her response to Marie, when asked how long before the State Department could expect reports.

Becky watched tutorial videos about using the new military laptop. It had been fifteen years since she used a military laptop, and it was less powerful than her home computer.

She told Daniel, "I thought I would only need to watch an hour of the videos, and I would be good to go. After all, I worked with computers in the Air Force and we even have a nice desktop unit at home."

"But this military laptop, with its triple encryption and security protocols, is more complex than anything I have ever used."

Embarrassed, and frustrated, Becky asked Marie to get a tech on the sat-phone to walk her through unlocking the laptop, after she entered the wrong code, and the system shut down.

After the tech helped unlock the laptop, Marie said, "Mrs. Draper you have been going at this for several days, and not progressing as fast as you would like."

"I suggest that you take a break, and take the rest of today off. Spend the time with your family, and come back at it refreshed tomorrow."

She felt the frustration was building inside, and knew that the rest of that day was not going to be very productive. Giving a loud-frustrated sigh, and putting her face in her hands, she said, "OK, you are right, it's break time. Please put everything in the safe, and I'll start fresh tomorrow."

Walking down a path with Daniel, with one guard several feet ahead of them, and one several feet behind, they enjoyed the walk the best they could.

This was truly the first time they had any "almost" time alone since arriving at the safe house. Daniel chose that moment to apologize to her.

"I am sorry I didn't tell you that I was still in the Navy. It's just that I didn't want to worry you..."

Becky interrupted, "You know how I grew up, and you know how well I served in the Air Force. How could you think I was so fragile?"

"No, it's not that I didn't think you could handle it," He said, "but I just didn't want you to have to deal with it if it wasn't necessary."

Becky stopped, turned to Daniel, and said, "We are in this together, no more keeping stuff from me – trying to protect me. Are we clear?"

With a big smile, Daniel said, "I hear you ten by ten."

After the walk with Daniel, and spending extra time with the boys and her mom that evening; she felt refreshed in the morning.

By mid-day, all of the preliminary training was done with no internet connection. Becky called Marie to the office, "I am comfortable with the laptop operations now, I will need to learn to navigate the online protocols. Please sign me in so I can become familiar with the laptop's working operations."

Marie retrieved the login information from the safe and logged Becky in. "OK, here you go. You will be allowed to upload the **Becky** software to the laptop, using the protocols you've learned."

"I have to leave the room while you are working with the software. It is well above my security clearance."

Once Marie left the room, Becky uploaded the current software updates. That was when she received a surprise.

*"Welcome, Becky, we are now **Team Becky"*** was the message that appeared on the laptop screen.

She gave a slight smile as she confirmed her security clearance and spent the next couple of days bringing herself up to speed with the progress of the spy ring investigation.

She reviewed all the available notes, messages, and memos in the "Eyes Only" pouch from the Deputy Director of the NSA. Now all of the information was in one place to be analyzed and assigned a security value for the first time.

Becky ran a summary report once the information was updated on the laptop. The Summary report was just to see what was known and what information was still needed. That was the critical security secret of **Becky**, the software, it would tell you what was required to produce a final answer.

She marveled at the advancement of **Becky**. When Becky left the Air Force, she had just started working on the codes allowing the software to ask for specific information.

"Look at you now." she said out loud, "to see you working is an absolute joy." As she made the required notes for command, Becky Draper started referring to **Becky** (the software) as **BTS**.

In her notes, she said, "I refer to **Becky** (the software) as **BTS** throughout this report. I suggest moving forward all references to **Becky** (the software) be **BTS.** It is best to separate the software from the person.

BTS provided information about the spy ring and how some known operatives were killed. Team Becky determined that there was a shadow person in a senior position in the State Department.

As part of her closing summary statement, **Becky** wrote, "...Although this person is closely associated with someone in authority, they were not necessarily in an authority position themselves."

The summary report assigned an alphanumeric value to each related and suspected event. For example, BTS would set a value for known associated events and suspected related events.

The report would also indicate the order of the events in the sequence of events and the importance of the sequence. The report would also make note of an event that was only suspected to be associated but not confirmed.

The event markers were new magic sauce software updates to Becky. Denise Terry was working on event identifiers when Becky Tyler left the Air Force. The report produced by BTS was the first time Becky saw the concept working.

Team Becky produced a mind-blowing report one week later and tied unrelated incidents together. For example, BTS linked the single-car accident involving a van on the interstate, I-

85 North, between Anderson, NC, and Spartanburg, N.C., to the shooting of Daniel.

BTS theorized that the driver, who was killed in the accident, was the person who shot Daniel and was killed as a loose end.

BTS also concluded that the man who died in a fiery single-car crash on I-65 North between Huntsville, AL, and Nashville, TN. was Eugene J Bullard, the spy who tried to get information from Denise Terry. He too was killed as a loose end.

The one unknown related event not in the timeline was the killing of police Sargent Andy Woodruff. It was not until the notes of Mary Rogers' interview with Jack Campbell were entered into the system that his death was associated.

A statement in the BTS report stated, "Although Woodruff was not a central figure in the overall scheme of things, his death offered a valuable clue.

With other deaths, there was chatter and scrambled sat-phone calls before the killings. With Woodruff, there was no chatter or scrambled sat-phone calls until after he was shot in the diner.

That meant someone in authority killed Woodruff because there was no time to get the work assigned. Everyone missed this important fact associated with the investigation.

As Marie, Jack, and Daniel gathered in the office discussing the Team Becky findings, Jack said, "Since we know that Mary Rogers was at the hospital when Woodruff was killed, so she is not the person in authority the report is talking about.

So, how do we zero in on the suspected leader?"

As Becky looked over the notes from BTS, she reviewed the new section which highlighted the unknown factors. "I have it!" she said, almost yelling. "We need to construct a general questionnaire, to be given to everyone associated with this investigation."

Marie said, "Wouldn't it be too obvious if people were asked for a timeline accounting for that day?"

So, Team Becky devised a questionnaire, asking people to account for their time in a fifteen-day bracket around Woodruff's death. These answers to the questionnaire would provide additional clues.

The killing of Bill and Pamela Smith was very telling. Once the memos from the Director of the NSA were added to the information, it was apparent that Pamela Smith killed her husband, and she was later killed as a loose end.

Based on the report from BTS, Pamela's association with the spy cell was tracked from the beginning of her employment with the NSA.

Early Wednesday morning, the FBI served a warrant on the food truck staff near the NSA building. As the truck was prepping for the lunch rush, and not paying attention to the people outside of the truck, 20 agents raided the truck. For the first time, one of the scrambled sat-phones was recovered.

Simultaneously while teams raided the truck, there were men with blue FBI wind-breakers, and AR-15 assault rifles raiding each of the employees' homes.

The white paper and the sat-phone calls associated with Pamela Smith were the information needed to get the warrants. When Ruby heard of the successful raids, she said under her breath, "Yes Pamela you were a spy, but you deserved better. This day is for you."

The captured sat-phone yielded a plethora of information. All of which were used to zero in on the heart of the spy cell. The FBI, NSA, State Department, and other alphabet agencies reviewed the intelligence recovered during the raid for the next several weeks.

The confiscation of the first sat-phone allowed the FBI to identify others, which allowed them to map out the historical locations of the phones and the locations of many of the phones they communicated with, including a sat-phone call made from the home of Bill and Pamela Smith, the night Bill fell in the shower.

Two things became very evident through the research of the information gathered. The first was that the spy ring was that of a friendly nation, based on the data collected and how the data was shared throughout the spy ring.

The second thing was that Becky Draper was indeed a target, she and her family were not safe. Protocol Clean Slate was truly needed to keep the family safe. They could never go back to their previous lives, and the same for Jack.

Becky Draper was finally ready to present a final report. She let Marie know that she needed to be able to present her findings to all the various department heads. Marie relayed the request to her command, which relayed it to the State Department.

This was out of the question, there was no way the State Department would allow Becky to come out of hiding to do a presentation.

Becky insisted that there be a group presentation. She also said that the group meeting itself would yield some information that could lead to the identification of the leader of the spy cell.

The Secretary of State and the NSA Director were made aware of the conversation about doing a group presentation. It was Daniel who produced a plan of action.

Daniel planned to send the boys, and Becky's mother, to the new secret permanent location. Becky, Marie, and Daniel would use a helicopter to fly to the group meeting location. He also suggested that the meeting take place in an airport hangar.

Marie suggested that only the Secretary of State and the NSA Director would know the true reason for the meeting. Everyone else would be told that the meeting was some sort of anti-terrorism training.

Marie explained that they would use sleight of hand, by flying in a helicopter to an airport and landing outside the hangar doors. Attendees of the meeting would all arrive in a collection of black SUVs.

After the presentation, while the people at the meeting stayed in their seats, Becky and her people would leave the hangar, pass through the doors, and head for the helicopter. However, they would get into a waiting SUV.

The helicopter would take off, and Becky, Jack & Marie would sit in an SUV parked near all the other SUVs of the group who attended the presentation. Once everyone started to leave, their SUV would blend in with the others leaving the airport.

Once they were out of the area, the SUV would take them to the new secret location. The plan was approved by the Secretary of State and the NSA Director, and the date was scheduled for Tuesday of the upcoming week.

The only item of concern was that Becky would be in the open for the first time since leaving the airport hotel. If the Team Becky report was right, then a leader of the spy ring would be there also, and wouldn't need to seek permission to kill her.

CHAPTER TWENTY-TWO

Fort Polk

The Director of the NSA, On Monday afternoon, sent emails to the following individuals: Mary Rogers, Robert Reed, Sally (The receptionist at the NSA building), William Johnson, Ruby Walker, Clay Wilkinson, and the Secretary of State.

The email informed everyone about the mandatory meeting. They were also asked to produce and bring a calendar, showing their daily activities for the 15 days listed in the email. The email concluded, "The State Department will supply your transportation. The meeting is top secret, please do not discuss it with anyone."

Everyone believed they were going to a mandatory secret training meeting, not expecting it to be a trap to flush out the head of the spy cell.

Private jets flew everyone to the Huntsville International Airport, and black SUVs drove everyone to hanger #24; the last hanger in the row of hangers on the private side of the airport.

Not only was the hanger on the blind side of the airport, the SUVs were parked on the hanger's blindside, and could not be seen by the rest of the airport.

Once inside the hangar, individuals had to put their cell phones and their activity calendars in a box near the door. Once everyone was seated, and ready for the meeting to start, Lieutenant Adams collected the participant's calendars from the box.

Ruby conducted the general meeting, while the Secretary of State, NSA Director, FBI Director, and the CIA Liaison had a private meeting for a debrief from Becky Draper.

Ruby spoke on the importance of the DNA database, and how it helped to identify a NSA employee, who had been killed, and bodies dumped without identification. She spoke on the need for more internal activity reports from lower-level managers to their department heads.

After Ruby concluded her statements, everyone was waiting to hear about the exciting new security they were there to learn. However, when the Director reentered the room, from the private meeting, he only spoke about the need for tighter security.

When the Director concluded the meeting, everyone had puzzled looks on their faces, and were asking each other, "What the hell was that all about?"

Everyone was held inside until the helicopter that brought Becky, Daniel, Jack, and Lieutenant Adams to the meeting had left.

Before the meeting, Marie questioned if it was wise to have Becky anywhere near the meeting, but Command did not share her concerns, so there were no changes to the plan.

Lieutenant Adam's only mission at the meeting was to collect the calendars. After she had collected them, she got into the last SUV. She was joined by the Drapers and Jack after their secret meeting with the NSA Director was completed.

The meeting attendees were allowed to exit the hangar and enter the waiting SUVs after the helicopter left. No one noticed that there was an extra one waiting with the others.

The SUVs were waiting to leave when a sat phone inside the last SUV rang,

"Go for Adams."

The NSA Director was on the phone, "Were you able to collect all of the activity calendars?"

Marie assured him, "Yes sir, I have them all, and everyone made it to the SUV unnoticed."

"Excellent Lieutenant. Now look in the glove compartment and take out the white sealed envelope."

Marie did as instructed, "Yes sir, I have it in my hand."

He then said, "Please inspect it and verify that it does not appear to have been opened, or tampered with in any manner."

Once she was satisfied, "Sir, the envelope is intact, and appears not to have been tampered with."

The Director responded, "Open it, inside should be two other envelopes, one is addressed to "Driver," and the other is addressed to you.

The NSA Director was walking out of the hangar door while he was on the phone to Lieutenant Adams, not knowing that someone was still in the hangar.

The person lagging, heard the part of the call where the Director asked about the calendars. He sat down on a nearby chair and started to think, *This whole meeting was just to get the calendars. Why would there be so much interest in people's schedules over those fifteen days?*

He thought, *What was so important about those days*? He focused on each day's activities on his calendar. One day stood out. *Surely that can't be it?* he said to himself.

"Reed, are you coming?!" Mary yelled from the door, "The SUVs can't move until everyone is in."

He waived and did a little trot to the door. Once they were in the SUV they were sharing, Mary asked, "What were you doing back there? We were all waiting for you."

Reed said, "I was confused, the meeting was supposed to be about learning new security information, but we didn't learn anything."

All the SUVs filed out in a single row, a couple took their passengers to the airport terminal building, allowing them to catch their private planes back to Washington.

Mary leaned over and said, "They wanted the calendars. That is the only thing I can think of. That was all we were asked to bring, and someone collected them while we were in the meeting."

Then Reed said, "Oh, OK." And he was quiet back to Washington on the private plane.

Lieutenant Ross, the driver of the SUV that held the Tylers, Jack, and Lieutenant Adams; was constantly checking his rearview mirror, looking ahead as far as he could see, and scanning his surroundings. Once he was satisfied it was safe, he pulled the SUV over to the side and parked.

He opened the envelope that Marie had handed to him.

The envelope had driving instructions and GPS navigation coordinates.

"Lieutenant, please enter the coordinates into your onboard system, and follow the directions to the next stop. Another driver will be waiting at the specified location. Your passengers will transfer to the new SUV.

Once the other SUV has departed, you are to wait in the location for one hour, to make sure no one is following, and that there are no potential threats."

The message in the envelope addressed to Lieutenant Adams said:

"Lieutenant, five SUVs and drivers will take your group to the new location. At each change location, the waiting SUV will have an envelope in the glove compartment. Pull the envelope out of the glove compartment, and inspect the envelope to make sure it has not been tampered with. Give it to the driver. However, if an envelope appears to have been

**compromised, open it and call the phone number printed on
the inside of the flap."**

The trip and SUV exchanges were uneventful, until the
fourth SUV. They pulled up behind the waiting SUV, and
everyone started getting out and collecting their bags just as
before.

Their driver stayed in his seat, unbuckled his seatbelt, and
unbuttoned his sidearm holster as standard security protocol. As
Marie reached the front passenger door of the waiting SUV, she
smiled and nodded to the driver.

She opened the glove compartment and pulled out the
envelope. She saw that there were signs that the envelope had been
tampered with.

Per her instructions, she opened the envelope and called the
number written on the inside of the envelope flap.

A female voice simply said, "SUV four, please hand the
phone to the driver."

Marie said, "It's for you." Handing the phone to the driver.
She then turned and said, "Everyone needs to get back into the
other SUV."

Becky and Jack started asking questions, and Marie gave
Daniel a look that said we are not safe. He said everyone should
just go back to the SUV and not fuss.

After the driver was through with the call, he handed the
phone back to Marie. She returned to the SUV they arrived in and
handed the phone to the driver. She said, "This call is for you."

The driver took the phone and said, "Yes, this is Lieutenant
Jones." After the call, he handed the phone to Marie and said,
"Everyone get situated and buckle In, I'm your driver to your final
destination."

Reaching into his door compartment, he took out an envelope and handed it to Lieutenant Adams. Printed on the front was, "Alt-destination." She inspected the envelope, it did not appear to have been tampered with.

She opened the envelope and inside were two more envelopes. One addressed to "Driver 3 – eyes only." Lieutenant Adams handed the envelope to the driver. He opened it and entered the new GPS coordinates into the navigation system. He said to everyone, "Go ahead and get some sleep if you can, we have a ways to go."

Lieutenant Adams opened her envelope, a little thicker than earlier envelopes. Inside was a two-page letter, which explained that she was reading the contents of this envelope because there were some security concerns with the fourth SUV. It continued with information about the new destination.

"Lieutenant Adams, your new destination is Fort Polk, in Vernon Parish, Louisiana. Fort Polk is a Joint Readiness Training Center, with lots of movement and a constant overturn of military and civilian personnel. This is important because the family will be posted there for some time.

Their new identity will start there, and the boys and their grandmother will be redirected there. The boys will be entered into a particular school designed to continue their education and aid them in adapting to their new identities. Their teachers will assist them in getting used to their new names and new family backgrounds.

The adults likewise will go through a process of indoctrination into their new identities. Also, Becky will set up the new "Team Becky" protocols. Yours and Master Chief's assignments are to keep everyone safe. You will receive added orders and chain of command guidance once you get to Fort Polk."

Lieutenant Adams put the pages back into the envelope, folded the envelope in half, and tucked it inside her blouse. As she turned to face her door, she got as comfortable as possible and said to the driver, "Make sure I'm awake at least thirty minutes before we reach Fort Polk."

The driver did not have to wake Lieutenant Adams in the end. He was about to when the Sat-phone rang. Marie sat up, adjusted her clothing, and answered the phone, "Go for Adams." She listened for a moment, said, "Yes Sir," and handed the phone to the driver. She said, "It's for you, the State Department is asking for a security sit-rep."

The driver thanked her and took the phone. "This is Lieutenant Jones. Yes Sir. THP35X. Yes Sir, thirty to forty minutes. Yes, Sir, I'll keep them safe." He pushed the end call button and handed the phone back to Marie.

Marie asked about the call. Jones said, "Just some Guy from the State Department, he said that with the security change in the destination, he wanted to make sure there were no other issues. He asked for this SUV's motor pool I.D. number and how close we were to our end destination."

The driver saw the look of worry on Marie's face, "No cause for concern. I have been driving these details for a while, it is typical for security check-in. We are asked to give the motor pool I.D. number because the whole number is not stamped on the vehicle.

The driver would not know the whole number if we were carjacked. If I were held at gunpoint, I would only give the number stamped on the vehicle."

Marie paused then asked, "That man's voice sounded a little familiar. What's his name?"

"I don't know, Ma'am, just someone from the State Department."

"Isn't it strange that the State Department would call for a sit-rep?

"Not at all, just depends on which department has the lead."

"But doesn't the NSA have the lead?"

"Ma'am, that is above my pay grade."

Marie turned and just looked out of the window. Something about the call just did not sit well with her, but the driver did not seem concerned, and there were no signs of any security issues. The call kept nagging Marie, so she asked the driver to pull over at the next safe spot.

With significant irritation in his voice, he said, "Yes, Ma'am, whatever you say. But we are only about ten minutes from the gate."

Daniel had been awake for a while and said, "Lieutenant, what's the problem?"

"It is probably nothing Master Chief, but my gut is churning."

"What do you want to do?" Daniel asked.

"Master Chief, since Fort Polk is a Joint Readiness Training Center, do you think your C.O. could have someone he can reach out to?"

"I could find out, but what would I tell him, Lieutenant?"

Looking out of the window, Marie said, "Tell him that the Navy fills something churning in her gut. We need a ride on the Q.T."

She took a pen and a piece of paper from her pocket. She looked at the navigation system and wrote down their present location.

She gave the sat-phone and the piece of paper to Daniel. He called his C.O., said what Marie had told him, and provided their location coordinates.

Daniel hung up the phone after speaking with his C.O. He said to Marie "The C.O. is sending a taxi to pick us up." He just laughed when he saw the look on Marie's face.

In about twenty minutes, they saw a giant sand-colored military vehicle with six wheels coming toward them. It stopped in front of the SUV, and the military transport driver clicked a mike connected to an external speaker. "You called for a taxi?"

By now, everyone was awake and looking through the front window of the SUV. "What in the world is that?" Jack asked.

Daniel said, "That is a Cougar 6X6 MRAP designed to maximize passenger survivability against small arms."

Daniel saw everyone looking at him, "I trained with Cougar."

Becky asked, "What does MRAP stand for?'

"Mine-resistant ambush-provided."

Following Marie's directions, everyone got out of the SUV. She told them to leave their bags, they would retrieve them when the SUV reached the fort.

The back door gate of the Cougar opened and two armed soldiers got out and took up defensive positions. One at the back of the SUV and one at the back of the Cougar.

Marie asked the SUV driver to wait thirty minutes before entering the base gates. After everyone was in the Cougar, the two soldiers standing guard got back in, and they headed back to Fort Polk. Marie had second thoughts and returned to the SUV to retrieve the calendars they had collected at the meeting.

There was a tiny window at the back of the Cougar, and Marie sat watching behind them. Within ten minutes, she saw the SUV following, "He did not wait as I told him to." She said to herself.

The driver of the SUV made sure he stayed well back behind the Cougar, hoping not to be seen.

After watching the SUV for a couple of miles, Marie decided not to end the driver's military career because he did not wait on the side of the road after driving most of the night.

Marie had looked away for a moment, and as she turned back to look at the Cougar, there was a bright flash of light, followed by a boom that shook the Cougar.

"It blew up!" She yelled, "The SUV Just blew up!" She said again.

Daniel and Jack joined her at the window, they watched through the back window, as black smoke, with an orange tinge billowed from the burning SUV.

CHAPTER TWENTY-THREE

The Investigator

The NSA's listening departments picked up a massive amount of chatter from lots of sat-phone calls being made. No one knew why there were so many calls or where the action was happening.

The NSA Director got the State Department, the FBI, and the CIA liaison on a conference call. He went through the mandatory security checks and issued a waiver for a secure conference call.

Frustrated that no one knew what was going on, he said, "Since whatever is happening affects all of us, I thought it was important for us to have this meeting call."

He went on to say, "I have a caller waiting to join the call, Lieutenant Marie Adams," after clicking her into the call, "Lieutenant Adams you are now connected by conference call to NSA, FBI, and CIA.

Everyone has been briefed on the SUV being blown up, and the actions you took while transporting the Drapers. Please describe what happened, and explain your actions."

Marie felt pressure building inside her and a tinge of fear. She had already been debriefed, so she was not sure why she was on this call. In a tone as professional, strong, and confident as she could, she began.

"First, let me tell you that you have a mole in the State Department. Since we now know of at least one that was in the NSA, we can be assured there are more, not just in the State Department. This person in the State Department is one of the leaders in the spy ring we've been chasing for nearly a year."

Marie stopped talking, she pushed the mute button, but hovered over it, as she waited in anticipation of questions someone on the call might have. There was complete silence, no one said anything – and finally, the Director of the NSA asked, " OK young lady, do you care to explain that statement?"

"Yes sir, I can," Marie answered with full confidence. "While we were en route to Fort Polk, after changing destination, and after not taking the fourth SUV, we received a call from someone claiming to be from the State Department for a security sit-rep.

For some reason, the call concerned me so much that I asked for transportation to be sent from Fort Polk…"

Interrupting her story, the Agent from the FBI clicked in. "Lieutenant Adams, did you see anything to support your suspicion at this point?"

"No, Sir," she said, "Other than the situation with the 4th SUV and envelopes. Everything was OK. I told the Master Chief later that I was not even sure the envelope had been tampered with, it could have been my eyes playing tricks on me."

The FBI clicked back in, "What do you think now, Lieutenant?"

Marie got close to the phone mic and said, "Hell yeah, I'm 100% certain now."

The Secretary of State said, "OK, everyone, take a five-minute break but leave the phones connected and on mute so signals won't be lost. When we are back live, I'll have two team members with me, Mary Rogers and Robert Reed. I think it essential to pull everyone in to get a fuller picture."

With that, everyone put their phones on mute and took a quick break.

The Secretary of State was the last to click in after everyone returned from the break. He said, "I have Mary Rogers with me, but Robert Reed was called to the Turkish Embassy, he will call in as soon as possible.

So, Lieutenant Adams, you already know Mary Rogers, I brought her up to speed where you left off. Please continue your debrief."

"Hello, Ms. Rogers. The last time we met, I was unsure of your motives. Now I believe you are one of the Good guys."

Marie proceeded to report what happened after the transport from Fort Polk arrived, and how she asked the SUV driver to wait a half hour before following.

When she paused, Mary Rogers clicked in with an empathetic voice., "But that was when things went upside down, right?"

Before she could respond, the NSA Director clicked in, "State, did you request the security sit-rep?"

"We did not," was the response from the Secretary of State. "We have followed up with all State personnel except one. He has been out of reach for a couple of days."

"Who is this person?" The FBI Director clicked in. "Is he a person of interest, a suspect, or what?"

The Secretary of State replied, "We have no answers, just questions at this point. However, within the next 24 hours, we will toss it over to the FBI if we have not satisfied our questions."

"Damn that, what is this Guy's name?" The NSA Director asked.

"Sir, I would much rather learn the facts before elevating his name." said the Secretary of State.

"In about one minute, the decision will not be yours, what is his name?"

The Secretary of State replied, "His name is Robert Reed; he partners with Mary Rogers."

"Isn't that the one you just said you could not get in touch with because he is at the Turkish embassy?"

"Yes, it is, but I want to give him a chance to explain himself, and..."

NSA Director interrupted State, "I want a BOLO (be on the lookout) issued in all 50 states, if we don't have him within 24 hours, I want a Red Notice issued through Interpol."

The Secretary of State argued "But Sir, to issue a Red Notice through Interpol, we must have conclusive proof of a serious terrorist or level one criminal. We already know where he's at; the Turkish Embassy."

The NSA Director replied, "We will let Lieutenant Adams finish, and then we will discuss this further. I'll provide some additional information to all of you. Lieutenant, carry on with your story."

"To be on the safe side," Marie started, "and out of respect for my Navy gut, the Master Chief had Fort Polk send transportation to us. About ten minutes after the call, a Cougar 6X6MRAP pulled up and parked nose-to-nose with our SUV.

We gathered our things and loaded them in from the back of the Cougar." She paused as she fought to maintain her composure.

"Do you need a break, Lieutenant?" The Director of the NSA asked.

"No, I can continue," she replied, "I asked the driver of the SUV to wait thirty minutes before following us to the Fort."

Taking another deep breath, she went on, "We were only about ten minutes down the road when I saw the SUV rounding a curve. At first, I was upset and going to have him busted, but thought better of it. After all, this poor driver drove all night to get us there, and I decided not to put him on report for not following my orders."

She then shared how she saw the SUV explode, and how the Master Chief gave the driver orders not to stop but to radio ahead for others to come out and inspect the SUV.

"The Master Chef also asked the driver to request direct communications to the C.O.'s office. Once the C.O. got on the horn, the Master Chief explained that his crew was in imminent danger and needed not to stop at the gate and be directed to a secure area on the base."

The NSA Director asked Lieutenant Adams to stop once she said that they entered the gate. "Lieutenant, there will be official debriefs from base personnel, and there were no other events on base. Correct?"

"Correct sir." With that, Lieutenant Adams muted her line, and the NSA Director asked Mary Rogers, "Ms. Rogers, have you been in touch with Becky Draper in the last 24 hours?"

"No sir, but I have her report findings with me."

"What findings, and why don't I know about them?" asked the Secretary of State.

The NSA Director responded to the question. "Mary was under direct orders from me not to share the information with anyone, including you. Sorry State, I was limiting access to the information, that's all.

Without discussing the report's source or the people involved, Mary, please share the findings with everyone."

"Yes Sir. According to the report the NSA Director is speaking of, Robert Reed is part of the spy ring we have been chasing for a year. On top of that, he may also be a leader in the ring.

I was able to pass this information on to the NSA Director just before joining this conference call."

"Mary, could you please tell the group what government Reed is working for?"

"Yes Sir, it appears to be Turkey."

With disgust and fire in his voice, the NSA Director said, "If we do not have Reed in hand within 24 hours, I'll issue the Red Notice through Interpol. State, you, and Mary grab lunch, and then both of you come to my office. Be here by 2:30."

The conference call ended.

Around 2:20 pm, the Secretary of State and Mary Rogers arrived at the NSA Director's Office. His secretary sent them to the Director's conference room. They were surprised to see Lieutenant Adams, Master Chief Daniel Draper, Jack Campbell, and Becky Draper.

The NSA Director ushered them inside "Come on in. We have a lot to discuss and a plan of action to put into place. First, thank you to Mary Rogers and Lieutenant Adams for expertly keeping Jack and the Draper family safe. However, Mrs. Draper's life is in greater danger because we proved that her program worked. Team Becky figured out that Robert Reed was the spy ring's leader and that he was working for the Turkish government.

The problem is, there are more of them because as soon as his name was known, he was called to the Turkish Embassy just before we could get to him. When we reached out to their embassy to talk to the Washington Envoy, she was unavailable. They told me she would be out for the rest of the week."

The Secretary of State added, "You know they'll have him out of the country tonight. He is as good as gone no matter what precautions we take."

"Yes, we know," said the NSA Director, "but our first mission is to ensure Team Becky is safe. We have already set up the Draper's and Jack's new identities and Becky's new office.

Lieutenant Adams will now work with Team Becky full-time, with Team Becky serving as a Government Contractor, making it easier to keep Becky safe.

Master Chief Draper will continue in Active Reserve, and his primary job will be to protect his wife and kids. Once you leave my office today, the transport team will take you to your new location with your new identities.

No one is allowed to know where you are or what your new names are. Lieutenant Adams will be your outside contact for Mary Rogers. So, any information you need will come through Lieutenant Adams and Mary."

Becky cleared her throat, "Yes, but there is one essential thing. Daniel needs monthly medical care and will need it for life, according to his doctors. Going to a V.A. hospital once or twice a year is not an option. What will we do about that?"

The NSA Director looked at Mary Rogers as if he were seeking an answer from her. She looked at Daniel, smiled, and said, "I already have a doctor in mind. We have to call him back to active duty, but Daniel will have his doctor within 30 days."

After another thirty minutes of general conversation, everyone reassured Becky that all would be OK. The NSA Director buzzed his secretary to send the transport protection detail to take the Drapers, Jack, and Lieutenant Adams to their new location. As they were leaving, the Director asked Jack and Daniel to stay back for a moment.

Once the office door was closed, the Director turned to Jack and said, "So, have you decided to take us up on the offer?"

"Yes, I've decided. I'll get him."

The Director looked at Daniel and said, "If you had to use a word or phrase to describe Jack professionally, what would it be?" Daniel looked at Jack, and without a thought, he said, "The Investigator."

The Director stuck out his hand to shake Daniel's hand. "Master Chief – Daniel, thank you for your continued service to our country, and I wish you well. Your only mission now is to keep your family safe. Jack will not be traveling with you today; he is needed elsewhere."

Daniel shook the Director's hand and then turned to Jack. "I take it you have already had a conversation with the parties that be, and you have agreed to whatever they have planned?"

Jack stepped close to Daniel and said, "Yes Bones, he tried to kill people I love, I'm going after him." With that, Jack walked out of the office and left the world he had known all his life.

It was 5:35 pm on a Friday when the receptionist buzzed Dr. Fredericks' office phone in the regional hospital in Huntsville, Alabama. The Doctor picked it up, "Yes, Mable, what is it?" The receptionist said, "Dr. Fredericks, there is a Mary Rogers on the line."

Dr. Fredericks clicked the lit button on his desk phone, and forced a smile, "Hello Mary, how may I assist you today?

"Call your wife, tell her to start packing. Your country needs you active again. The government packers will be at your home Monday, you will be moved out and on your way to your new location by Friday."

With that, Mary hung up the phone without giving the Doctor time to ask any questions or to protest.

Jack met with the CIA Liaison, and he was taken to an undisclosed location, where he spent the next six months training with CIA field operatives. His natural investigative abilities were enhanced, and his body ached because of the physical developmental training.

It was a Tuesday morning when his training officers said, "Jack, from this point on your code name will be The Investigator. Pack your go bag, and give the Secretary of State a call. Good luck to you."

When the Secretary of State answered the phone, Jack said, "This is Jack, I understand you asked for me to call you."

The Secretary let out a big long sigh, and said, "We found him, it is time for the Investigator to go to work. The particulars are been sent to your phone."

The Investigator said, "I understand." And he hung up the phone.

Four months later, an "Eyes Only" pouch from the CIA to the NSA and State Department confirmed that the FBI had made major arrests, and dismantled the espionage ring. The report concluded, "One Robert Reed, after tendering the information needed to close down the spy ring, was killed trying to escape."

Made in the USA
Middletown, DE
02 September 2024

60289891R00135